What the critics are saying…

"*Slave Castle* is an incredibly well-written story!...Claire Thompson delved into the minds of both submissives and dominants in this sexy romp...I highly recommend "Slave Castle" to any reader who is looking to take a walk on the wild side of romance." ~ *Adrienne Kama The Romance Studio*

"If you like bondage and domination, *Slave Castle* is an exceptional read...This is a great book and I highly recommend it." ~ *Laci Grey Just Erotic Romance Reviews*

"*Slave Castle* is well written, with the evolution of Marissa throughout her training and her living life on her own terms...If you don't mind handcuffs and whips, pull up a chair and read Slave Castle!" ~ *Jenni ARR (A Romance Review)*

CLAIRE THOMPSON

Slave Castle

ELLORA'S CAVE
ROMANTICA PUBLISHING

An Ellora's Cave Romantica Publication

www.ellorascave.com

Slave Castle

ISBN # 1419950622
Cover art by: Syneca

Electronic book Publication: December, 2003
Trade paperback Publication: June, 2005

Warning:

The following material contains graphic sexual content meant for mature readers. *Slave Castle* has been rated *X-treme* by a minimum of three independent reviewers.

Ellora's Cave Publishing offers three levels of Romantica™ reading entertainment: S (S-ensuous), E (E-rotic), and X (X-treme).

S-e*nsuous* love scenes are explicit and leave nothing to the imagination.

E-*rotic* love scenes are explicit, leave nothing to the imagination, and are high in volume per the overall word count. In addition, some E-rated titles might contain fantasy material that some readers find objectionable, such as bondage, submission, same sex encounters, forced seductions, etc. E-rated titles are the most graphic titles we carry; it is common, for instance, for an author to use words such as "fucking", "cock", "pussy", etc., within their work of literature.

X-*treme* titles differ from E-rated titles only in plot premise and storyline execution. Unlike E-rated titles, stories designated with the letter X tend to contain controversial subject matter not for the faint of heart.

Also by Claire Thompson:

Sacred Circle

Secret Diaries

Jewel Thief

Face of Submission

Seduction of Colette

Slave Gamble

Slave Castle

Trademarks Acknowledgement

Chapter One

"No! I won't do it!" Marissa's lip trembled but she stared defiantly at Tom. "You can't make me!"

"I don't want to make you," Tom said quietly, his voice rigid with self-control. Marissa was naked, kneeling on her knees in front of him. Her arms were wrapped around her torso in a protective gesture and her eyes were flashing. Tom sighed. Things weren't working out with Marissa, which was a shame because he had to admit he was enormously attracted to her and desperately wanted to own her.

Looking down on the impossible, gorgeous creature at his feet, he sighed. Marissa's hair was thick and loosely waved, copper-colored in the flickering light of the many candles lit about the spacious master bathroom of Tom's penthouse. It was that hair which first attracted him at the party. It wasn't auburn exactly, and certainly not red. No, if it had to be defined, it was copper, burnished with gold and lustrously tousled now. Her skin was smooth and soft, and her eyes were large and dark as she glared up at him, daring him with her expression.

When she *wanted* to submit, when he "ordered" her to do what suited her, Marissa could be very submissive, or at least compliant. When he shackled her facedown to a whipping board, legs lewdly splayed on either side, pussy spread against the leather-covered wood so he could whip her with his new heavy-tressed whip, she obeyed without hesitation. And her moans and cries were so sexy as each blow from the whip forced her little pussy against the leather, the lovely sting of the whip mingling so deliciously with the mounting friction against her clit.

When he ordered her to kneel before him naked and hold perfectly still with her mouth open like a little bird she did so, her eyes sparkling with anticipation. She was like a statue of a goddess as he fucked her face, impaling her so that he knew she couldn't breathe until he pulled back enough to allow it.

But now as he demanded something she didn't already want to do, something that would actually require *submission* and not just the satisfaction of her masochistic and sluttish nature, she balked. As with each other task or idea he devised that didn't meet specifically with her own desires, she had resisted, and then refused him. When he had wanted to fuck her ass, Marissa had demurred, telling him she never "allowed" a man "back there".

At first he had been challenged and he had gotten a thrill from holding her down and "forcing" her. He had taken her virgin ass and she had cried out and struggled, but she had orgasmed, screaming his name and he had realized pretty quickly that what she was after was the fight. She *wanted* him to present suggestions and ideas she would refuse so he could then "force" her to obey.

And it had been fun, at first. What a wild two weeks they had had since that first night he had brought her home. They had barely left the house, so focused on exploring each other that their bodies were raw from the passion, literally sore to the touch, and yet, still the flame seemed to burn in him for her.

He still experienced a delirium of desire when their bodies came together and he could feel her sweat-slick breasts and belly flattened beneath him. It was as if a bolt of electric current ran through both their bodies and would only release them from each other when it ceased, leaving long, shuddering waves of pleasure in its wake.

They had met at his friend George's house where she had assured him she was submissive and wanted—no, was longing for—a "real" master to take her in hand. She had come with a group of girlfriends, but she had left with him. Against his own better judgment, Tom had taken her home that very night. What ensued could barely be classified as a Dominant/submissive love affair. From the beginning it was more of a fight, with him demanding obedience and her refusing, or daring him to "make her", which he would usually do, subduing her through sheer force. It had been exhilarating, leading to wild and clashing sexual encounters that left them both completely spent.

In a word, it was fun, but it wasn't what Tom was seeking. It was a game and clearly that was what this mysterious young woman was interested in. A game of cat and mouse where the mouse was completely in control.

Tom, on the other hand, wanted a truly submissive sexual slave who would obey his every command and comply with his every whim, however outrageous. Someone who would kiss the whip after he used it to flog her, someone who would live for the chance to serve him and ache for his tender words.

Somehow Marissa had burned her way under his skin in a way that was very rare for Tom who liked to think of himself as surrounded by an invisible sheet of ice that kept others at a proper distance. How had she slipped under the ice? When he'd met her at the party, he had been ready to leave. Normally Tom was aloof at those events. His friend George held them several times a year at his country estate in Orange County. The guests were discreetly served by a household of slave girls and boys who saw to everyone's comfort, and also served as the evening's entertainment if the guests weren't sufficiently titillated with each other.

Tom casually enjoyed the parties, the freely flowing fine champagne and the buffets piled with gourmet foods. The naked and semi-naked servants silently glided about the rooms, serving food and graciously submitting to the gentle and not-so-gentle fondling by the guests. He would usually pick a slave girl or two and take them off to an adjoining bedroom for a little rough play and sex. But it meant nothing to him. He wouldn't ask their names and he rarely thought of them again afterwards. It was just a diversion, a relaxation after a hard week investing the money of certain wealthy New Yorkers, which was what Tom did for a living—a very lucrative one.

Now on this late spring afternoon, Tom sat on his balcony overlooking the city. He was nursing a gin and tonic, a rueful smile playing on his face. Marissa was still asleep in his big king-sized bed, sprawled naked across the satin sheets. After their second day together, she had essentially moved in and at the time Tom hadn't minded. She didn't seem to have a job and told him she was "between careers". She didn't elaborate and he hadn't pressed. For the moment it had been enough to have this nymphomaniac angel-slut in his bed.

Now he was growing restless. At thirty-four, he found himself longing more and more often for something more than the one-night stands or the two-week stand this little adventure had so far turned into. Marissa wasn't his dream girl, at least she didn't behave like his dream girl, his slave girl, his submissive angel. He didn't want a little hellcat, however beautiful and erotic. This wasn't going to work, he could see that. Why postpone the inevitable?

He would tell her. He would tell her now.

"Marissa!" Tom called through the screen that separated him from his bedroom. No response. "Marissa! Wake up. Come out here. I need to talk to you."

"You come in here," came her sleepy mumble.

"No. I want you out here. Now." Something in his tone must have made it clear he meant business, because a moment later a sleep-tousled and naked Marissa came sauntering out, pushing her hair from her face, totally relaxed in her nudity.

"What, baby?" Her voice was pleasingly low, still husky from sleep.

"I've been thinking, Marissa." Tom leaned back in his chair, shading his eyes as he looked up into Marissa's lovely face. The sun was behind her and he couldn't see her features. "Sit down," he said abruptly. She sat across from him on an overstuffed rattan patio chair, crossing her long, bare legs.

"What have you been thinking, Master Sir?" This was Marissa's nickname for Tom. At first he had liked it, thinking she meant it as a term of respect. It had become clear though that this was her private joke. She was her own master, no question of that.

He pursed his lips a moment, wondering how blunt to be, and decided to hell with it. "That it's time for you to leave. It's been really fun, Marissa, but we both should be getting on with our lives now."

Marissa stared at Tom for a second and then threw her head back, her laugh full-throated and deep. "You silly," she said. When he didn't join in her laughter, but merely regarded her impassively, Marissa's laugh faltered and faded altogether. She paled and her large dark eyes seemed to grow even larger.

"But, Tom," she began, her voice higher pitched than normal in her distress. "Why? We're so good together. Please! You're kidding, right? Say you're kidding." Her eyes pooled with unshed tears and she knelt in front of him, wrapping her arms around his waist. Her bare breasts pressed sweetly against his knees.

Despite himself, Tom felt his body respond to her touch. Something about her electrified him, he couldn't deny it. But she wasn't for him. He knew this with certainty. She wasn't what he had dreamed of. He steeled himself against her touch and pried her fingers loose, forcing her to let go of him.

Marissa hugged herself, still kneeling naked in front of him. "What did I do, Tom? Did I offend you somehow? Please tell me. Let me fix it! I'll do anything. Anything to stay."

Please, I love you.

She didn't say that, and Tom suddenly realized it was what he was longing to hear, what might have weakened his resolve and have made him want to keep trying with her. But she didn't say it. She had never said it, though to be fair, neither had he.

Sure she wanted to stay, who wouldn't? She lived in a cramped apartment on Broadway with three roommates. She had no job and no steady lover. Why wouldn't she want to stay in Tom's penthouse overlooking Central Park where a maid cleaned every morning and a cook made their meals when they didn't dine out?

Tom knew that part of his charm, indeed perhaps most it, was due to his wealth. His looks were nothing to speak of, certainly not in his own mind. About five ten, Tom had a narrow build, slim with long, lean muscles and narrow hips. Glasses usually hid his rather beautiful brown eyes and his dark hair was thick but fine, falling in a straight fringe that frequently got in his eyes. He didn't have a problem dating women, but he was never sure if they were attracted to him or to his money, and this only added layers to the ice he kept around his heart.

Tom stared at her, none of these thoughts articulated until Marissa began to cry quietly, pretty little tears that welled over dark eyes onto smooth cheeks. Her tears tore at him, but Tom wasn't to be so easily manipulated. Abruptly he stood up. "Listen, I need to clear my head. You can stay here 'til I get back. We'll talk some more, then. I'm sorry, I just can't do this anymore. It's a game for you, but I need more." He left her, still kneeling naked, thirty stories above the teeming city, her head buried in her arms.

Tom didn't go far. One block over and two blocks down in a small, undistinguished brownstone nestled between large glass buildings was a discreet private club, which sported the small sign over its locked doors that said simply "The Club". Again, it was his friend George McBride who had invited him to join this exclusive group of self-professed dominants who lived or worked in the city and came here to unwind in traditional and less than traditional ways. The Club had the usual bar and tables for casual relaxation and conversation. But it also had a fully equipped dungeon, available by appointment for Doms and their submissives to explore their lifestyle in private or public as they chose.

As luck would have it, George was there now, sitting alone at a table, sipping a Bloody Mary and watching a football game on the wide-screen TV, which covered most of one wall. He gestured a greeting as Tom stood at the entrance of the club, his eyes adjusting to the dim light. Responding to George's unspoken invitation, he joined his friend, sliding into an empty seat as a waitress appeared to take his order.

Small talk was exchanged, though Tom couldn't have told you a minute later what either of them had said. A gin and tonic appeared, smelling sweetly of fresh lime. He took a long drink before leaning back in his chair, staring moodily at the game on TV, seeing nothing.

"So what's up, Tommy?" George asked, his voice hearty and a little too loud in the intimate atmosphere. "You seem rather out of sorts. Your newest toy break or something?" He laughed and winked, but Tom didn't smile back.

"I guess you could say that," he said, the image of Marissa's tear-stained face crushing his heart like a vise.

"You're talking about the girl with the hair, right? The one you left the party with? That was your first mistake, old boy. Taking her home without checking her out first. Dangerous to think with your cock, though in her case I can't say I blame you!" George laughed suggestively. "She crashed my party, you know. I found out later she didn't have an invitation, but with a bod like that who cares, right?" Again the wink and the insinuating grin, which normally wouldn't have bothered Tom at all, but for some reason today irritated him.

George plowed on. "So what happened? Did she find someone better? Or did you? Or are you just tired of that particular piece of ass and coming 'round here for a new one?" George laughed, his expression a leer of implied complicity.

Tom sighed, passing a hand over his forehead, pushing his hair back, though it immediately fell forward again. He was barely paying attention to George, but needed the chance to say aloud what had been torturing his mind for these several days now.

"Her name is Marissa, and no, I'm not tired of her, at least not physically. It's something else. I need more. I'm not so young anymore." He broke off as George started to protest. George was a good five years older than Tom and still behaved like a teenager with no intention of "settling down" in his game plan.

"No, please, George, you know what I mean. I want more. I want a soul mate. I'm tired of this casual sex and the loneliness the next morning, wondering who the person next to me is and what they're doing there. I need a connection. I need a lover, someone who fits my groove, who is submissive to my dominant will. Who not only understands what I need but longs to give it. Lives to give it."

He stopped talking, realizing it was hopeless, foolish even, to share these deep feelings with George. George was the consummate party animal. And as Tom should have expected, he laughed derisively and said, "Tommy, Tommy, always the romantic. When will you ever learn? There's no such thing as a 'true submissive'. Your so-called slave girls only exist in erotica novels and porn movies. In real life there's just sluts looking for a good time. They all just want to get off in an exciting new way. And they want to do it in style, which we give them in spades, don't we, Tommy boy? In spades."

Tom looked at George, at his heavy face twisted in a conspiring grimace, the fleshy cheeks that would soon be sliding into jowls, the small, pale eyes, close on either side of his smallish, upturned nose. There was high color in George's cheeks and Tommy realized he had probably had quite a few Bloody Marys before Tom joined him. He recognized suddenly that he really didn't care for George all that much.

They had a long history together, having started out as roommates in graduate school, both hot to get their MBAs and make a killing in the financial markets, which both of them had done with a vengeance. And while they shared a penchant for submissive women and whips and chains that was really where their connection ended.

Tom retreated at that moment, inwardly angry with himself for having divulged his own pain to another man. He changed the subject to "George", which was easy to do as George's favorite topic was George. "Forget all that stuff. I'm just tired," Tom said, forcing his voice to a lightness he did not feel. "Tell me about you. What're you doing here today?"

"Thought you'd never ask. I'm meeting two hot little numbers in a few minutes, down in the dungeon. One is a professional dominatrix, and she's bringing me a new toy. A highly trained submissive slave girl who I'm gonna pay good money to play with and abuse. She takes a good beating, I'm told. I can beat her 'til she bleeds if I want to. Of course, I'm paying her Mistress, not her. She's the object, I plan to be the subject." He grinned, obviously pleased with his clever turn of phrase.

Tom answered, "A submissive, huh? But you have to 'buy' her, so it's just a game."

"So what? It's all just a game to me. You know that. I know, I know—" George put up his hand defensively, "—for you it's 'real'—a 'way of life'. You want a 'relationship' with someone who will completely subjugate her will to yours. Well, good luck, buddy. I think that's just fairytale stuff personally, but whatever floats your boat."

Tom said nothing, refusing to engage in the discussion, but silently wondering if maybe George was right and his expectations were ridiculous. They watched the game on TV for a while and then George waved over the waitress, settled his tab and said, "Well, Tommy, I'm off to have some serious fun. My girls are waiting for me." Tom watched his friend, a large man whose substantial muscle was just beginning to turn to fat, lumber toward the back exit, which led down to the dungeon.

Tom sipped his drink, holding the cold glass between his palms, thinking of Marissa and his own foolish dreams. He started when someone said, "Excuse me, but may I join you?" Looking up, Tom saw a slim, rather short man with dark hair, cut short and a pleasant face, nose a trifle prominent, eyes kind and smiling.

Tom gestured toward the empty seat, curious as to who this person was. He hadn't seen him here before, which surprised him as the clientele was select and rather small. Membership fees naturally excluding most from its ranks.

"Thank you," the man said, and Tom observed a very slight accent, more noticeable as very precise pronunciation than as an actual identifiable accent. It was slightly British in pronunciation.

"Allow me to introduce myself. My name is André Renaud." He stuck out his hand and Tom automatically took it, noting the firm grip.

"Tom Reed."

"A pleasure, Mr. Reed," André said, as he slipped gracefully into the offered seat. "I couldn't help overhearing a little bit of your conversation with your friend. Please forgive me if I am overstepping but as we are all of a like mind here—" he gestured vaguely around the room, clearly suggesting they were all "Doms" here and rich ones at that. Tom noticed now the fine cut of the man's suit and the emerald cufflinks, which were no doubt real.

"Not at all," he answered, wondering what was coming, assuming it had to do with money, as most things did.

"I do not mean to intrude, but I did hear what you were saying. About the longing for a connection, something real with a truly submissive woman." Tom colored slightly, embarrassed to have been overheard in such a vulnerable moment.

The man went on. "I only trouble you because I have the same feelings, the same desires, and know how difficult it is to make such a connection. Very few people are 'true submissives' as you say. Very few are born to it, but it is my humble opinion that they can be 'made'."

Tom looked at him, confused. "I don't follow you."

"I mean they can be taught. If a person—man or woman—has certain submissive tendencies, they can be taught to submit in a way that is pleasing and proper. Even if they have already exhibited clearly submissive behaviors, these behaviors can be refined and enhanced with proper training. On the other hand, if they are willful types—brats—I call them, who like a good fight and to be overpowered, they can be instructed in the art of submissive behavior. And in time, they come to actually incorporate that submissiveness into their natures. A good slave can be made, Mr. Reed." He sat back, clearly expecting a response.

"That's interesting. I'm not really sure what you're getting at, though." What was the man selling? Tom had a nose for salesmen, and this was one, however refined and elegant he appeared.

"Forgive me, I am not being clear. Specifically, I run a little business." *Ah, now for the pitch.* "I prefer to think of it as a calling, really. A vocation. I have a small estate near Westchester that I've turned into something which might be of interest to a man of your tastes. A man looking for a 'true submissive' as I believe you said."

Tom pursed his lips, waiting for an offer to use this fellow's escort service, no doubt for a hefty fee. Though already skeptical and ready to dismiss the man, he listened politely, despite the caution bells in his head, as André elaborated.

"My little dream became a reality a number of years ago. I run a little establishment called Chateau L'Esclave."

"Slave Castle," Tom interjected, having minored in French in college.

"Indeed." André nodded, a smile of approval on his face. "It is a very select establishment set up for the training of slaves of the highest caliber. Most of the slaves there already belong to a master or mistress, and have been sent to us to hone their submissive skills. We accept slaves anywhere from a week to a year, depending on their master's particular needs and desires. Slaves are trained in all of the submissive arts, up to the highest standards developed here and in Europe by some of the most prominent and successful trainers in the business. And, of course, we work closely with the master to make sure their needs and desires are incorporated in the training."

Tom wasn't aware there was such a "business" but he refrained from comment, further intrigued despite himself. "We also have slaves for sale. That is, they have a contract, which can be purchased. The sales price and contract terms are negotiated with all parties, including the slave. In fact, most of the monies go to the slave, with Chateau L'Esclave naturally taking a fee.

"The slave is part of the negotiations, since though they are completely submissive and 'owned' by their master or mistress, said ownership is completely voluntary. I suppose you could say the slavery is really a 'fiction', since slavery on its face is illegal. But it becomes very real indeed, with the exchange of power nonetheless binding, despite it being consensual.

"We also have a permanent staff of trained slaves who serve the house with complete subservience. I say permanent, in that they live there, but, of course, in fact they are free to go."

Tom interjected. "Wait a minute. Let me get this straight. You're saying you own this *slave castle*? A place where real people live 'the life' 24/7? Where people send their girlfriends and wives for a little slave training? Is this legal? Is this for real?"

"Completely legal and absolutely real." André smiled, sensing he had caught Reed's interest at last. He sat back, lacing his hands over his slim stomach. "It is all voluntary, no one is there against their will. I have an excellent attorney who has meticulously researched our options, and prepared contracts and disclaimers, which fully protect all parties."

Tom's mind was racing, turning naturally to Marissa. Would she consent to such "training"? Would it make a difference? He had to know more. Anticipating his concerns André said, "If this seems like something you might be interested in exploring, I would be delighted to set up a personal tour. I suggest only you coming first. If you have someone in mind who could use a little training, we would bring her along later.

"She would, of course, have to be totally comfortable with the program. It would never work otherwise. We have an excellent program for the 'brats'. You would be amazed at the change we can effect with the right, ah, incentives." He smiled, his eyes twinkling.

"And certainly, as I mentioned, we have slaves 'for sale'. Right now I have two very promising submissive young women who need placement. You could look them over if you like, as well."

Tom started, suddenly entertaining the possibility of a slave for purchase. The stuff of fantasies, surely, and yet, here was this dapper man, calmly informing Tom of his options in the slave market! He felt a little disloyal stab as he thought of Marissa, whom he'd left at home crying, waiting for his ultimatum to allow her to stay or force her to go.

Never a man to give away his intentions, Tom was noncommittal as he accepted Renaud's card. "I'll give you a call," he promised, now eager to get home to Marissa and at least float the idea with her. He realized the little flare of hope that had surged up in him was an indication that Marissa meant more to him than he had been willing to admit. He had to have her, but on his terms. Pocketing the little business card, he took his leave.

Back at the apartment Marissa was waiting, dressed now in a little sundress that made it clear nothing was underneath. Her nipples poked sweetly against the soft fabric, her breasts raised by her arms crossed protectively under them. Her copper hair tumbled around a face bare of makeup, with eyes reddened from crying. She sat curled in one of his large leather chairs, looking like a lost little waif.

"Marissa—" the word was wrenched from his lips as he crossed quickly over to her, kneeling at her feet, dropping his head into her lap, "—I'm sorry, honey. I'm sorry. I didn't want to make you cry. I just can't keep on how we're going. I don't want the games anymore. I need more."

"What do you want, Tom? Tell me what you want? I'll do it. I'll do anything." Tom felt her cool fingers smoothing the hair from his forehead.

"I want something I'm not sure you can give. And it isn't fair for me to ask it. I want a submissive slave girl. Not a willful sex kitten, I'm sorry. You are incredibly sexy and fun, but it isn't what I want in my life right now."

"Oh, Tom! I can change! I swear I can. I can be what you want! I want to be what you want. I want to be with you." Her voice was pleading, almost a whine.

Until that day, he would have rejected her promise outright. He didn't believe one could "make a slave" as Mr. Renaud had staunchly affirmed. He believed it was an orientation plain and simple, and while a slave could be "trained", they could not be molded into something they were not. And yet here was his darling Marissa, so beautiful and vulnerable, pleading to keep a place in his life. Who was he to make the decree that she couldn't try?

And so, ignoring the little voice inside of himself that said it would never work, he decided to take a chance. Producing the little business card from his pocket, he silently handed it to Marissa.

"What's this?" she asked, taking it. "Chateau L'Esclave—by appointment only," she read. "What's that? Some kind of castle, right? Why are you showing me this? Is it a restaurant?" And so Tom explained about his meeting with the Frenchman, and about this supposed slave castle where they could take someone like Marissa and turn her into the woman of his dreams.

Instead of being offended that he wanted to change her thus, as he had half expected, Marissa seemed excited, even eager. "It sounds exotic!" she said. "An adventure! I mean, it's safe, isn't it? They won't, like, hold me hostage or anything?"

"Not according to this guy. He said it's all on the up and up. Strictly legal with contracts and the whole bit. But I would want to go out there and check it out. See if I think it's something we would be interested in. If you're interested, that is. I certainly don't want to force you into this, Marissa."

"Would you be with me? I wouldn't have to go alone, would I? Is it a real castle? Are there servants?" Marissa was sitting up straight now, looking as eager as a new kitten for a ball of twine. Another delightful game for this little Cinderella.

Tom smiled despite himself—she was impossibly charming. "I really don't even know what it is. It could be a big sham, or a cover-up for prostitution or who knows what. But, I'm willing to go take a look, if you're interested."

Marissa looked at Tom through a thick fringe of lashes, consciously coquettish, her mouth a sweet little pout. "I'll do anything for you, Tom. Anything at all." She pressed her arms together, no doubt aware of how it pressed her breasts up and together to create a deep and alluring cleavage. His penis responded, now totally shushing any remaining little warning bells as he took her in his arms, as firmly ensnared as ever.

Chapter Two

To get to Le Chateau L'Esclave one had to travel along a meandering lane, a ribbon of pavement that snaked back and forth as it angled upward into the foothills. Massive branches of live oak hung out over the road. There were no other houses visible. The driveway extended perhaps a quarter of a mile to a proper English manor house at the far end, a three-story Tudor with a steeply pitched slate roof.

As Tom pulled into the circular drive, a valet was instantly at his side, opening the door of his Lexus, bowing slightly as Tom got out. Tom thanked the man who parked the car nearby while Tom looked around him.

The place was a large stone house, probably hundreds of years old but beautifully restored and maintained. It was dove-gray granite and the pigeons strutting across the pavement looked as if they'd been placed there purely for their decorative effect. Even the sound they made was refined, a low churring murmur. The door was flanked by big copper urns oxidized with streaks of blue, planted with delicate birches in bud.

"Please Enter" a small signed discreetly advised. Already impressed, Tom pushed through the doublewide door of carved mahogany, the upper half inset with glass. The front room was built on a grand scale, flooded with light from two translucent glass skylights that created a gracious sense of space.

A young receptionist looked up from her desk at the foot of the stairs. "You must be Mr. Reed," she said, smiling. "Please have a seat, sir. Claudette will be with you shortly." As she spoke, the young woman pressed a button on her telephone. A moment later a tall, imposing woman dressed in flowing silk, her feet bare, her long hair swept back from her face in a satin ribbon, appeared at the top of the stairs.

"Ah, Monsieur Reed," she smiled, gliding toward Tom, holding out both hands, taking his in hers and clasping them as if he was a long-lost friend. "Such a pleasure to meet you. I am Claudette, Claudette Rodin. André has told me all about you."

Unlike André, Claudette's accent was thick, with the pure vowels and rolling Rs in the back of her throat, which marked her as thoroughly French. Tom saw that her hair, which he had first taken for blonde, was in fact white, the lovely silver-white certain women were lucky enough to achieve naturally as they aged. Clearly once a great beauty, even now she had a structure of bone and smoothness of skin that made many a younger woman envious.

Her face was lined with good humor around the mouth and eyes. Tom found himself liking her immediately. "Please, call me Tom," he said.

"Very well then, Tom," she smiled broadly, though in her mouth it came out as "Tome". "Let us become better acquainted, you and I. Anne!" She turned toward the receptionist, her voice sharper as she addressed the young woman. "Bring us refreshments on the back veranda, please." As Anne hurried away, Tom observed that she, too, was barefoot, which he found rather peculiar, though he did not comment aloud.

Claudette led Tom through a large room furnished with old-fashioned pieces, large blue- and white-striped couches and ample reading chairs. Two of the walls were covered floor to ceiling with books, the others held pictures of pastoral landscapes in oils and watercolors. It looked like a room where one could spend many a peaceful afternoon. He noticed the books actually looked used — they weren't the usual rows of books purchased by some interior decorator at auction, matching leather-bound books no one had ever read or intended to read. These had spines that had at least been opened, and he stifled his natural impulse to go over and see what this massive library contained as he hurried to follow the mistress of the house.

Through French doors Tom was led to a long wraparound veranda. A row of chaise lounges lent it the look of a ship's deck. Under a canopy of oaks, the ground sloped down gradually, leveling out then for a hundred yards until it met the road. On the left, in an area cleared of trees, he caught a glimpse of a small lake shimmering in the sunlight. Two tennis courts were also visible through the oaks.

The petite young woman named Anne appeared as the two of them settled into the comfortable chairs. As she set the tray of drinks and little cakes on the small table between them, Tom was startled by a very clear view of her pretty, round breasts, completely bare and now showing as her little tunic fell open.

Claudette grinned at him and said, "Eyeing the goods, I see. No, no, don't apologize! It's quite all right. She exists for our pleasure, don't you see. She is an object to be enjoyed."

Tom had started to protest, embarrassed for himself and for Anne, but Anne didn't seem to be embarrassed. She stood passively, eyes down, a small smile whispering at her mouth. "Of course you are not used to us here, Tom. I forget you have not even had the tour. I'll give you a small sample of what I mean. Anne," again the sharp tone. "Lift your dress for Monsieur Reed."

Without hesitation, Anne lifted her dress over her head, like a three-year-old playing with her clothes. She was completely naked beneath, her delicate, pale body smooth, marked only by two gold rings, one through each nipple. Her mons was covered by a soft little triangle of dark blonde hair. Tom felt his face flush, and at the same time his pants became uncomfortably tight.

"Very nice, dear. You may go." As Anne smoothed her dress back down and left them, Claudette continued, as if this sort of thing happened all the time. "Anne is a slave, of course. She is a house slave. She isn't here for training. She lives here full-time. She belongs to the house. She's for sale, actually, though André tells me that is not what you are here for."

Tom licked his lips, his mouth suddenly dry. Claudette offered him some of the fresh peach iced tea, which he accepted gratefully, using the moment to sip it as he collected his thoughts. Was this place for real?

Claudette saved him the necessity of responding, as she continued. "Let me formally welcome you, Monsieur Reed, to Le Chateau L'Esclave. André has told me you may have a client for us. A headstrong girl in need of refinement. Let me assure you, this is the place for her. Before I show you around, let me tell you some things about us." As she spoke, Claudette arranged her skirts with white fingers that stroked the silk delicately, he could almost feel its rippling softness himself, as if it slid cool against his own skin.

"We have several programs, each carefully designed over years of experimentation and experience in training people to be proper slaves. Of course, each program is tailored to the specific needs of the individual and to the desires of their masters.

"But on a general level, there are three types of submissives here. First is what André calls the 'brats', but I prefer to call them the willful ones. These are girls who are used to getting what they want. Girls who use a pretense of submission to gain control of their lovers. Girls who pretend to submit but actually wrap men around their little fingers."

"Sounds like Marissa," Tom said, grinning.

Claudette's laugh was rich, the sort of laughter you have to join in with even if you have no idea what is funny. Casually she adjusted a few white narcissi sitting in a slender jug on the table, their fragrance as sharp and clean as spring rain.

"Yes, André had mentioned she might be in that first category. These girls frequently misbehave and often their masters, though in love with them, are at their wits' end on how to control them. We train the girls, and we train you as well. We will give you the tools to keep your girl on her best behavior once she has completed her training here. We teach her humility and submission. We will display her, humble her, teach her to serve in all things with grace. For many of these girls, this is the first time in their life they are not the center of attention and specifically the center of sexual attentions.

"Second we have the true submissives, the ones who are already inclined but need assistance. They are here because they don't yet meet the standards their masters wish for them. Not everyone is equipped or inclined to train their personal slaves, but that doesn't mean they don't have high standards. I'm sure a busy man like yourself well understands such a situation."

He did indeed, aware of her subtext that they would do the training and he would do the paying. Still, money really wasn't an issue here and he was beyond intrigued.

"And the third type?" Tom asked, affecting a casualness he did not feel. She had hooked him and surely knew it.

Claudette smiled, offering him a plate of freshly baked fruit tarts as she crossed her bare legs under the flowing silk of her long dress. "The third category of slave we have here are the discards, if you will. The ones who have been cast off by their masters or mistresses for one reason or another. They belong to the house. They do not share the same rights and privileges as the girls brought to us for the elegant training in the art of erotic slavery. No, these slaves usually come to us via a master who is tired of them, and they basically 'sell' them to us for a fee.

"They don't sleep in the lovely, private bedrooms I'll be showing you. The ones where your darling Marissa would be housed, should you choose to send her here. No. They sleep in a dorm in the basement of this place. They assist in the training of the slaves, where appropriate, and serve as our cleaning staff. They are also the house whores, to be used sexually by any and all who wish to use them thus. They are, in the truest sense of the word, slaves."

Tom looked stunned. This went far beyond the glamorous idea of sexual slave training for millionaires and their girlfriends. This sounded dangerous and definitely illegal.

Claudette read his concerns in his face and offered, "The lovely irony here, Monsieur Reed, is that it is all completely voluntary. No one here is 'forced' to stay against their will. The arrangement is not as formal as the one with those we train professionally. In return for their absolute service and devotion, we give our slaves a beautiful place to live, and much more importantly, the lifestyle they crave. If it doesn't work out, if either side is discontent with the arrangement, we wish them farewell and that is that.

"And, in fact, our house slaves are also paid a small salary as well for their services. They don't have access to the funds while they are here, but it is meticulously accounted for and kept in their name when they are ready to retire. House slaves rarely stay longer than a few years. We only have two who have been with us longer, and they are entirely devoted and will probably stay as long they are allowed.

"Not everyone is suited to this life, even those who think they are submissive and think they crave the life of a slave. And for many, even those who are truly submissive and derive great satisfaction from serving here, love does eventually enter the equation." Claudette smiled, her eyes crinkling at the corners. "There is love here, but not all the house slaves are especially cherished by a particular master, and that can come to be lonely. However, for those who long for absolute domination and control, for whom it is less a decision than an admission of what and who they are, there is no greater satisfaction."

She spoke with such conviction at that moment, her eyes shining, her cheeks faintly flushed, that she might be speaking for herself. Was she a slave in this bizarre establishment? He didn't feel comfortable inquiring.

Instead he asked, "If, just hypothetically speaking—" and Claudette nodded, a small smile still on her face, "—if I were to bring my, um, slave girl, that is, Marissa, to this place, how would it work? How long is the training for? I gather she stays here alone, which won't go over too well, I don't think. Not that I can blame her!"

"Yes, she would stay alone. After extensive discussion and consultation with you, during which time a proper program would be tailored for Marissa, she would be left here to begin her training. The average stay is two to four weeks, though some slaves stay much longer. It is a very personal decision on the part of the owner and the slave.

"Only by submersion in the program can she really feel free to shed all her past willful ideas of her own behaviors. If she thinks you will be popping in every day, she will be less inclined to 'give in' if you will. When a slave realizes there is no way out, she is more likely to pay attention and learn the lessons presented to her. I know this from years of experience, including my own."

Tom was again piqued by this hint of information. Claudette must be a slave, too! Perhaps she was one of the two she obliquely referred to as permanent house slaves. The idea intrigued him but good manners forbore comment, at least at this point.

Now she stood, tall and regal, silk flowing like water against her voluptuous form. "And now, Monsieur, if you have been refreshed, the tour. I will explain more as we walk." Tom again noted her beauty, and the fact she must be close to sixty seemed irrelevant in the face of her natural grace.

He stood, too, brushing any possible crumbs from his pants as he followed Claudette from the porch and back through the library. As they walked Claudette said, "First I'll show you where your slave girl would be sleeping, if you choose to bring her here."

They entered the large foyer where Anne was busy over some papers on her desk, entering data into a computer. She smiled demurely at Tom, and he smelled a sweet fragrance of lavender as they passed her. He stifled an impulse to touch her long, soft hair as they moved past her desk and up the large curving stairway.

Claudette led him to a room that was, at present, empty. It contained a large bed canopied in pale blue netting, which was held apart by large blue satin bows at each corner, tied prettily to the brass bedstead.

Oddly, there was nothing else in the room. No bureau, no chairs, no pictures on the walls, which were painted a creamy pale yellow. There was a large window, flanked by heavy curtains that swept the ground, looking out over the garden and sloping rolling hills of the estate. The curtains fluttered slightly as a breeze wafted through the open window.

Claudette explained. "This room is available at the moment. As you can see, there is only the bed right now. A slave girl begins with the bed, because we want her well rested, but she has to earn other things, such as the right to wear clothing, a place to keep that clothing, the privilege of a chair or table, or a book to read or music. And of course, these privileges can be taken away when the slave is disobedient or fails in some respect to meet the wishes and demands of her trainer."

"The right to wear clothing?" Tom asked, his expression one of surprise and disbelief.

"Tom, dear, you must realize what we are discussing here. I don't believe André has properly explained. This is not a summer vacation for spoiled young wives to be pampered and played with. This is serious training for women who are willing to completely subvert their own desires and needs to that of their master.

"Your Marissa, should you choose to send her here, will be stripped upon arrival, and she will not be permitted to dress until she has earned the privilege. She will be used, according to your dictates, of course, physically and sexually, to teach her her place. She will be punished, but not only because she misbehaves. She will be taught to crave the whip, the cane, even an erect penis however it is offered and whenever it is offered.

"This is not a game, Monsieur Reed, but a serious proposition, and an expensive one. If you deliver Marissa to us, it will be for real, but what you get back will be the girl of your dreams. You will have not only a submissive and subservient slave, but also a trained lover on par with the geishas of Japan and the finest courtesans of European royalty. We know what we are doing, sir."

Tom could well believe it. He found the image of his Marissa arriving here, stripped bare and forced to service another man as wildly erotic. Perversely, the thought of "giving her away" to another man, of watching her submit to another's base whims was a powerful aphrodisiac. He wished he was home just now, because he would take her, roughly, and not mind a bit if she fought him.

"Come, I'll show you some training in process. Slave Theresa is learning about the cane today. She is especially afraid of the rod, you see, and must be taught to submit with grace. She is a 'true submissive'. That is, she already yearns to bend completely to her master's will, but she lacks self-control. And she lets her own fear get in the way too much of her desire to obey.

"We are teaching her to get over that nonsense. Her master has chosen a four-week time frame, which should be ample time to bend her to our ways. Let me just check if it's all right for you to observe." They had walked down the hall and Tom thought he could hear faint cries behind a heavy oak door. Claudette knocked and opened the door, shutting it behind her, but not before Tom heard a feminine cry and a "Please! I can't!"

A moment later the door opened again and Claudette gestured. "Come in. Aaron says you may watch. They've been at it a while now and the lesson is almost complete. Theresa is not doing terribly well at the moment, but Aaron doesn't want to take her too far, as her fear is clouding her judgment."

Tom entered the room behind Claudette, half afraid of what he was going to see. The young woman named Theresa was standing at a bar running midway along the length of one wall. The wall was mirrored and the effect was like that of a ballet classroom. Theresa was naked and bent at the waist, her back to room. But because of the mirror, Tom could see her face, partially obscured by blonde hair falling in waves over her shoulders.

Her eyes were squeezed tight, tears running down reddened cheeks. Tom's eyes were drawn back to her naked body, her little curved bottom thrust out, its olive skin lined horizontally with dark pink welts.

Tom was shocked, realizing he had walked in on a caning, a real caning. Tom had fantasized often about caning a woman but had never had the courage, or the right partner to try it on. What he saw now went beyond submission in his mind, this was brutality, plain and simple. This was abuse!

Aaron no doubt read the shock in Tom's face and was used to it, because he smiled slightly and said as the cane landed once more neatly across her tortured behind, "You've never witnessed a caning, I presume? These marks will have faded by the end of the week. No skin broken, no lasting scars. It's just a caning. No different than a whipping when done properly, though I daresay it stings a good bit more, doesn't it, Theresa?"

Theresa squealed as the cane hit her tender flesh yet again but she remained in position, small hands tightly gripping the wooden bar. Her legs were trembling and even as his cock strained against his pants, Tom had an urge to run over and rescue her. Claudette's gentle grip on his forearm kept him where he was, however.

Aaron was tall and well-muscled but lean, his sandy blond hair pulled back in a ponytail, a diamond earring glinting from one lobe. His tanned arms were covered in a down of golden hair, contrasting nicely with his white linen shirt rolled up to just below the elbow. His voice was low and very precise, his diction perfect. Tom detected a decidedly British accent.

"Theresa lacks grace at the moment, as the cane frightens her unduly. She wants to obey, but fear is still overriding the need to submit. This poor little poppet has a way to go. Don't you, sweetheart?"

"Oh, please! Please, Sir! I'll try harder. I'm sorry! It hurts so! I hate the sound of it. I'm afraid!" Theresa was slight, with a thin little frame that put one in mind of a delicate bird. She looked so small and defenseless there, bent over the rail, naked and trembling.

"Hush," Aaron soothed. "Remember, this isn't about you. It's about what your master wants, and he wants you to learn to take the cane without all this crying and screaming. I know you know better. Have you forgotten that you exist solely for your master? I am his right hand now, Theresa. He has given me full authority over you. And I want to cane you. Isn't that enough for you or do you require more?"

"It's enough," she whispered, her voice breaking in a sob as his cane sliced through the air and landed on her thighs. Claudette pulled gently on Tom's arm, leading him reluctantly from the room.

"My God," he said as she shut the door on the poor woman's cries. "That was barbaric! That was beyond training or whatever you call it! He was really hurting her!"

Claudette laughed gently, and said, "Of course, he was really hurting her, Tom! Don't you understand that she craves the pain? As much as she fears it, she needs it. She wants it. She is not only submissive but masochistic. And she longs to please her master who is also her husband, and whom she adores beyond all reason. He adores her, too, but has never used the cane on her. He wants to take her to that new height of pleasure and pain, but is afraid himself. So he brought her here to learn. And he himself has also had a few lessons, practicing on one of our worthless house slaves.

"When Theresa leaves here, she will have learned to submit to a caning with grace. She will take a beating that will leave her marked, and she will not only submit to it, she will exalt in it. And she and her master will be able to rise to a new level together in their relationship, to something they couldn't achieve on their own."

"But the cane," Tom still protested, though what she was saying made sense. He himself had never dared wield a cane, perhaps a lesson or two...

Claudette seemed to understand Tom's reservations and his reluctance as he imagined Marissa bent over the rail as Theresa had been. "Remember, Tom, that this training you just witnessed was expressly developed for Theresa. Your Marissa's training would be especially developed for her, by you and her trainer who will also be Aaron, I believe. Aaron is especially gifted with the willful ones. He knows how to break them without breaking their spirit or their essence. He can help you to mold Marissa into the perfect submissive without taking away her fire."

That was it! That was what he wanted. Submission, but with fire! He didn't want a "Stepford Wife". He wanted a real and passionate woman who would submit to his wildest demands with grace and humility. He wanted what this bizarre place seemed to promise. Was it possible? Could money really buy his secret dreams? Would Marissa really agree to whatever they dreamed up for her?

"Let us visit the slave quarters before we go, Monsieur. We will talk more, and of course Michael is waiting to meet with you when the tour is over." Tom followed, his head crowded with images of the naked Theresa, of Anne lifting her dress, of Claudette herself, her ample bottom alluring in the soft silk as she walked in front of Tom now. He was fairly sure she was as naked as Anne beneath her gown. And the bare feet. Claudette must be a house slave! A house whore?

Wasn't that her word? House whores to be used by anyone who wanted to? Did that include the "masters" who paid so handsomely for the services of the house? *My*

God, he chastised himself, *you're thinking about fucking a woman at least twenty years older than you!* And yet his eyes slid back to her long feminine body, the silk sliding like water against bare buttocks and firm legs.

This place was getting to him! He swallowed, forcing himself to get a grip and quit fantasizing about making love to this woman old enough to be his mother! They walked down the large curving staircase again, past the desk, which was empty now. Where was Anne? They entered the large kitchen, which was filled with gleaming stainless steel appliances and wide butcher-block counters of softly polished blond wood.

Two people, a tall woman with long dark brown hair and a rather short man of no particular distinction, were chopping vegetables and stirring pots on the large gas range. The food smelled wonderful, of garlic frying in olive oil and tomatoes and some kind of meat, perhaps lamb.

They stopped speaking as Claudette led Tom through the room and she ignored them so Tom presumed, rightly, that they were servants. They both were dressed in soft cotton clothing. The man, in his mid-thirties, was short and rather stocky, his face nondescript. He was wearing pants and a heavy T-shirt, and again, he was barefoot. The woman, tall and robust, in her twenties, was in a cotton shift that opened at the neck, revealing the tops of full, mature breasts. The already aroused Tom found himself wondering if she, too, was naked beneath the little dress, and he concluded as he saw her bare, long legs and feet that she probably was. He nodded politely and they both nodded back, the man smiling, the woman looking down and licking her lips, a slight flush on her pretty cheeks.

Claudette led him down narrow stairs, nothing like the broad, sweeping staircase in the main part of the house. These were clearly servants' quarters to which they were descending. They came into what must have been a refurbished basement. Six bunks lined the walls, three on the bottom, three on the top, with little ladders. All the bunks were empty at present, and each bed was made with military precision, the little coverlets tucked smoothly over thin mattresses. A threadbare cotton throw rug lay over a clean stone floor. Against the far wall Tom noticed with a little shock that there were iron manacles rather like those in a medieval dungeon screwed into the wall. There were three sets of these manacles with cuffs for both wrists and ankles.

Claudette followed his eye and said, "That's right, Monsieur. As you are no doubt deducing, sometimes our bad little slaves must be punished. These are for the house slaves. We have also found it to be an excellent reminder during training. That is, with your prior permission, of course.

"Yes," she continued, clearly warming to her subject, "a night spent shackled here and you won't soon disobey again, I can assure you. Should anyone in a position of authority be displeased at anytime, for any infraction, they can order a slave to the dungeon wall. Occasionally they'll shackle someone just for the effect. It is a very pretty look, to see a naked young woman tethered here, breasts pulled high, body marked from a recent whipping, perhaps blindfolded, perhaps gagged."

Tom was silent, finding his throat seemed almost closed. The images she provoked in his mind disturbed and excited him. He saw Marissa there, her burnished hair gleaming in the light of a torch, her naked body slick with sweat, her eyes bound in black silk, her mouth silenced with a gag. He licked his lips and took a breath, annoyed with his runaway imagination.

"Quite a layout you have here, Claudette," he said, his voice brusque with repressed desire. "How many house slaves are there, anyway?"

"We have five at present. We are training two women right now, and holding the third spot for you. We only train three at once, as we have found that is a good number for our small staff. There is only me, Aaron, Michael and André. And, of course, the house slaves. You saw two of them in the kitchen. Amy and Scott."

"Scott! A man."

"Yes, men can be submissive, too, naturally! He, interestingly enough, used to consider himself dominant, and actually came to us to train his girlfriend. He realized in the process that it was he himself who had the submissive nature. She left the training before it was complete, but he ended up staying on, entirely of his own volition. He's been with us for two years now.

"And Amy was rejected by her lover. He gave her away basically because she is willful and has a roving eye. She wasn't faithful to him and he'd had enough. He signed her over to us. She could leave at any time but, again, she has chosen to stay. She is used most harshly by Michael and André, but it suits her. She is lent out for training periodically but so far no one wants to own her. That is, no one she is willing to go to. It has to be consensual, naturally."

"And Anne?" Tom asked, his heart curiously skipping a beat.

"Ah, Anne. Anne's story is an unusual one. She was brought here, via the traditional route of her master bringing her for more training. But instead of returning to him when the training was over, she asked to stay." At Tom's questioning look Claudette continued. "It was strange, as I say, but apparently her master was not her lover, not in the truest sense. Theirs was strictly a Dominant/submissive relationship. He controlled her, owned her body, dictated her sexual life, used her for his pleasure, but did not love her, nor she him.

"From my own observation, that sort of relationship doesn't last. For what is sexual pleasure without the added intensity of love? Ultimately it is nothing, a wisp of a dream, a taste of something with no sustenance, no abiding satisfaction. I suppose Anne came to feel the hollowness. Something in her experience here, perhaps, led her to believe there was more, that she needed more to be fulfilled. She asked for and was granted release from her bond to him. Her master didn't believe there was a place for love in such a relationship. To him, control and domination excluded love."

"He's not alone in that belief, you know," Tom said. "Lots of people feel that way. People who don't really understand anything about it, the ones who confuse 'abuse' with a loving and willing exchange of power, they think this whole 'whips and chains' thing is a perverse expression of hatred for women or something like that. They don't have a clue."

"You are correct, Monsieur. They miss the point, as you say in English. They fail to see the poetry of romantic submission. But this man, he did have an understanding of the exchange of power, and the willingness and joy with which Anne was eager to give herself to another. But for him, love was viewed as a weakness. If he loved her, he couldn't dominate her properly. So in a way, he was as eager as she to break the bond. In fact, he purchased a slave from us, someone who shared his philosophical view and as far as I know they are happy together."

"So Anne stayed here?"

"Yes, she stayed as a house slave. She has continued in some aspects of her training and in serving the house as required. She has a contract available, that is, she is for 'sale' but it's quite specific. She and Michael wrote it, and love is very clearly specified as a requirement. Love on both sides. She is quite the romantic." Claudette smiled, making it clear she approved of Anne's romantic ideas.

"But come. Let me take you to Michael. He can answer all your questions so much better than I." As they passed through the kitchen this time, Tom felt his own face color as he glanced sidelong at the two people he now knew for certain were house slaves. Busy at their pots, they didn't appear to notice.

Claudette knocked quietly at the door of what appeared to be a study located off the library. "Come," a deep voice issued from within. Claudette opened the door and then stepped back, gesturing for Tom to enter first, which he did. The man who must be Michael stood up and held out his hand to Tom. His handshake was firm and warm.

Michael, perhaps in his late fifties, wasn't an especially tall man, but the impression he gave was one of girth, of strength. His brown hair was longish and combed straight back. His temples were graced with a hint of silver.

His features implied someone big and strong, large dark eyes, a rather bulbous nose, slightly crooked, probably broken at least once, a large, generous mouth. He was wearing a pale gray suit from which peeked snow-white shirt cuffs with a pale blue monogram, hand-done, no doubt.

Smiling faintly, Michael took a flat cigarette case from his inside jacket pocket and extracted a slim, black cigarette that he tamped on the case and then stuck in his mouth, flicking a gold lighter.

"Mind if I smoke?" he asked, after the fact. He offered the case to Tom as he gestured for him to sit down.

"Not at all," Tom said, though he himself declined the offered case. He took in the man, observing his broad chest and shoulders, the muscles not completely hidden even under the perfect cut of his suit. He noted the large, blunt fingers—a workingman's hands, which seemed to belie his fine clothing and fancy cigarettes.

While Michael put away his cigarette case, Tom gazed about the room, which was warmly decorated in dark greens and rich browns. One wall was lined with old-fashioned, glass-fronted oak bookcases. Shelves were covered in knick-knacks and stacks of books, giving it a lived-in, cared-for look. The large desk at which Michael sat was covered in papers and more books. It was the kind of room Tom could enjoy working in and it made him instinctively like this man.

Tom noticed Claudette had not seated herself, but remained standing by the door, her face down, eyes on the floor.

"Come, *ma chérie*," Michael said softly to her, and Claudette came at once and knelt at Michael's feet. She seemed so natural there, kneeling on the floor as she lay her head delicately against his knee. Michael absently stroked her hair as he smiled down at her. Tom could see at once that they must be lovers.

"Has Claudette given you the tour, Mr. Reed? I am sure you have as many new questions as those that have already been answered. What are your impressions? What do you think of this fine establishment of ours?"

"I honestly don't know what to think," Tom said. "It's pretty amazing. It doesn't seem real. It's like a fairy tale or a romance novel come to life."

"Oh, it's very real, Mr. Reed. We have trained slaves here to do our bidding. Perhaps you need a demonstration. Perhaps you've deduced that my Claudette here is a slave? Yes, I can see by your face you know this. Isn't she lovely? Who better to use to show you we are serious indeed?"

Tom swallowed, a part of him intuitively ready for what was coming, yet still he was shocked when Michael continued. "Claudette is my personal slave girl. She belongs entirely to me, don't you, darling?"

Claudette whispered, "*Oui*, Michel. *Complètement.*"

Michael caressed her silver hair. "Shall we show Mr. Reed what an obedient little slave girl you are, Claudette, my love?"

"If it pleases you, sir," her voice was low and rich, full of promise. Tom unconsciously gripped the arms of his chair, his mind curiously blank.

"How about it, Mr. Reed? Let's be blunt here. You are skeptical, and I would enjoy proving to you that we deliver what we promise. If you wish, we can turn your girlfriend—Marissa, isn't it?—into a completely submissive slave girl as Claudette here is."

His voice was gentle, but the authority in it was iron-sure. Tom was embarrassed for Claudette he realized, because of her age. It was unseemly to have an older woman be treated thus. Michael seemed to read his mind, saying, "Please don't insult Claudette by assuming that because she is mature she is not sexual. As you can no doubt see, she is an extremely lovely and desirable woman. She submits to no one but myself, unless of course, I direct her.

"And I choose at this time to direct her to submit to you. What would you like, Mr. Reed? What can Claudette do for you? What is mine is yours."

Tom blushed, uncomfortable, crossing his legs to hide his erection as his body understood the implications of what Michael was offering before his mind did. Michael smiled at him, waiting, but Tom didn't know what to say. He could almost feel Claudette's soft tongue wrapping itself around his cock.

Claudette, still kneeling at Michael's feet, placed a hand on his forearm, her expression perhaps conveying that Tom was not ready for what he offered. Nodding, as if she had spoken aloud, Michael amended. "Forgive me, I am being gauche. You are not used to our ways and I forget that. Of course, you're not comfortable to have her submit sexually to you with me in the room! I have spent too many years in Europe I'm afraid, and I forget the delicate sensibilities of Americans. Let us settle instead for a simple demonstration. Claudette!"

"Sir?"

"Stand up and strip, and show Mr. Reed your beautiful body." Without hesitation, Claudette stood up and reached behind her neck, releasing the buttons that held her dress in place. Gracefully she stepped out of it, letting it fall to the floor, revealing her full, lush figure. For the second time that afternoon, Tom was presented with a naked woman who stood for his inspection. It felt surreal.

Which didn't stop him from looking. Claudette's large breasts were capped with pointed dark nipples, which now rose becomingly to attention. Her belly was curved and full, not fat, merely rounded in a feminine way. Her hips were fecund and inviting, rolling back to her ample bottom, which was now displayed as she turned slowly for the men, putting her hands up behind her head to give them a clear view.

Her expression was serene as she turned back to face them. Tom marveled at her calm and grace at showing herself like this in front of a total stranger. "Show him your sex, slave," Michael ordered, his voice still soft but edged with steel.

Tom stared as Claudette lifted one leg, placing her bare foot on a chair, angling herself so Tom could see her little pussy peeking out, a glint of gold on one side. "She's pierced, naturally. All slaves should be pierced somewhere. I decided Claudette's ring should be at her sex. Her nipples are too beautiful to mar. I did it myself, didn't I, Claudette?"

"*Oui*," she whispered, her cheeks now a becoming pink.

"It hurt, didn't it, slave girl? But you held still and spread your little pussy for me to drive the needle through, didn't you?"

"*Oui, Maitre. Oui. Tout pour vous.*" Her French was sweet, her voice low. Tom was mesmerized by what he was seeing, by her complete submission to this man, and his own strong physical reaction to this beautiful woman.

"You may leave us, Claudette. We have matters to discuss." Gracefully Claudette retrieved her dress and slipped from the room, closing the door with a tiny click.

Tom sat silently, as if stunned. "You are affected, I see," Michael remarked.

"I'll say," Tom admitted. "What I wouldn't give for that! God, what I wouldn't do to have Marissa submit to me like that! Not what she did so much as *how* she did it. The grace. The obvious pleasure, even *joy*, she took from submitting to you. It had nothing to do with me, I could definitely see that. It was very personal—intimate. I guess I'm surprised you shared that with me."

Waving his hand dismissively, as if it were nothing, Michael said, "You can have that, Tom. We can teach Marissa to give you what you deserve as her master. We've got a good track record in that regard, provided that that is what she truly wants. But we'll need carte blanche. The most successful training occurs when no limits or restrictions are placed on the trainer. While we would never harm your slave, we need to know we can do whatever we think is necessary to bend her, to mold her, to what she needs to become. That means we will whip her, though of course, leave no permanent marks. That means we will use her sexually, in any way we see fit, not for our pleasure but for her enlightenment. Nothing like hands-on experience, if you'll forgive the little pun."

Tom looked earnest, too intent on the enormity of what Michael was saying to even smile. "Do whatever it takes," he said. Had he been totally honest with himself, while the nobler part of him claimed he was giving Marissa the chance to learn to be the submissive lover she claimed she wanted to be, a baser part of him was angry with Marissa for withholding herself in the truest sense. Instinctively he knew she withheld her heart, even though her actions and words seemed to promise so much.

She had not been willing or able to submit to him on his terms so let these "experts" teach her a thing or two. He couldn't quite believe he was sitting here calmly discussing handing over his girlfriend to be whipped and fucked by strangers. What kind of man was he himself? Could he really love her as he claimed, and yet be willing to just give her away?

But he realized even as these questions flitted through his mind that he had bought into what these people were offering. His dream, the longing for the "perfect submissive woman" had been so piqued, so fired, by this bizarre day that he felt he would give anything to get it. And that baser part of him actually was delighted with the idea she'd be "put in her place" at last. God knows, she'd put enough men in theirs!

When Tom left, a full two hours later, his mind was made up. His brain was reeling with what he had heard and he was excited about the training program they had developed together. Michael, very official, had taken notes on his laptop, creating a simple but detailed plan of training for Marissa, all with Tom's input and support. The man who would be Marissa's primary trainer, Aaron, was called in for consultation and discussion. It was very like the business meetings with high-powered executives Tom was used to in his work. But the subject at hand was anything but familiar!

When the matter of money had come up, for Tom it had become a formality. As he wrote out a sizable check, which he left with Michael as a deposit, he knew he desperately wanted this now, no matter the price.

The only question was, would Marissa?

Chapter Three

"You're sure about this."

Marissa nodded, though she wasn't. One thing she *was* sure of, she didn't want to go back to her cramped little apartment with her stupid roommates and a lousy job waiting tables or temping in offices. It wasn't that she didn't like Tom. She did like him, immensely. He was rich, sexy and kind, and most importantly — rich.

Tom stared straight ahead, concentrating on making the right turnoff from the freeway that would lead them to the country estate where he was going to introduce Marissa to this fantasy-island situation of training little slave girls to serve their lords and masters.

Marissa looked over at him, reaching up long, slender fingers with perfectly manicured pink tips to lightly graze the back of his neck. "I want to please you," she whispered, her voice low and husky, completely aware of the effect it had on him.

Tom glanced at her then back at the road, smiling slightly, his expression unreadable. He had told her all about this so-called slave castle, where women and sometimes men were "trained" to learn to be proper submissives. He had explained until she felt her eyes glaze over about what his dreams were and how they included her, but only if she could learn to become what he wanted — no, what he demanded — in a woman.

Marissa didn't have a problem in theory with what he wanted, though to her it was still just a game. She found Tom cute in his intensity but also sometimes a little scary. At first he had loved the fight, the rough play, "forcing" her to do his bidding, and she loved it, too. It was thrilling to be overpowered by a man, to be forced to bend to his will and do all sorts of terrible, wonderful things. She had been in heaven those first two weeks, loving his constant attentions, the mind-blowing sex and all the fabulous accoutrements that went along with being with someone who was ridiculously wealthy.

But Tom, the romantic, had wanted "more". He'd basically told her to hit the road, and in that instant she had realized she might actually feel more for Tom than just a good time and a meal ticket. It took her a few days to figure out what his definition of "more" meant, but when he came back from that castle thing, he was so excited she knew she would be able to swing whatever it was and get back in his good graces.

She'd managed to hang out with rich guys before but they'd always been older, and not nearly as sexy as Tom. They quickly bored her, and though she liked the creature comforts, she wasn't shameless enough to stay when nothing was left but the room service and the fur coats.

As far as love was concerned, what the hell was that? She knew people professed it, but it wasn't part of her vocabulary, active or passive. It didn't seem to be part of Tom's either, which was a relief, since he didn't say it all the time, like some of them, and expect her to parrot it back. And yet, he did seem to care a lot about her. She had gotten the impression this place they were going to was not cheap, and he was willing to shell out the money for two weeks worth of "training".

Marissa shivered a little and shifted in the soft leather seat next to Tom. She adjusted the seat belt so it fit better between her round little breasts, wondering if Tom noticed how nicely her nipples poked against the sheer fabric of her little silky dress as the cool air-conditioned breeze reached them.

Training. He'd patiently explained they would be teaching her about the finer aspects of learning "grace" — whatever that was — taking a whipping, and learning fancy sexual techniques and body massage.

They were going to "train" her to be a first-class whore, from the sound of it. Marissa didn't say that, of course. She had nodded and murmured assents as Tom tried to explain about the contract she would sign, and about how she didn't have to go through with any of it if she didn't feel comfortable. He told her he would be a phone call away, she was to keep her cell phone charged and handy, and he'd call her every night.

She had balked at first when she'd realized Tom wouldn't be there for all this stuff, but then the thought began to intrigue her. Never a "one-man woman", Marissa had always enjoyed the attentions of a number of men at once. While she knew Tom was a good thing and planned to hang onto him as long as possible, the thought of open permission, indeed even an order, to "submit" to other men, all in the line of proper submissive training was immensely appealing. She could have her cake and eat it, too!

"What are you thinking?" Tom asked, smiling at her as they idled at a red light, not far now from the chateau.

Marissa hadn't realized her smile had reached her lips, but she quickly said, "How lucky I am. That you want to take the time and trouble to teach me like this. To help me learn what I can do to please you." Her voice was warm, sincere. She knew Tom had excellent "bullshit" detectors and she never laid it on thick with him, if she could help it. And in fact, she wasn't being totally insincere. She was appreciative that he was sending her to this luxury spa for two weeks—to tone up, to learn cool, new sexy techniques, to get a whipping from some "real Doms" as Tom called them.

Marissa was in fact sexually submissive or at least masochistic, and a good whipping got her seriously hot and ready for very intense sex. The way Tom described it, she'd have a two-week vacation, eating gourmet food, swimming and playing tennis, having wild sex with sexy strangers and also pleasing him by doing it! Not too bad for a twenty-five-year-old girl from the Bronx with no family, little education and fewer prospects!

"Wow," Marissa said, as they drove up the long, winding drive to the old stone mansion. "This is some setup! Like something from an old movie set or something. Is this for real?"

"Wait until you see inside! But remember, you're not committed to anything, that is, until you sign the contract Michael has written up for us. But Marissa—" he pulled in the drive now and turned toward her, "—this isn't a game. If you sign that thing, you're in it for the duration. I don't want you just trying it out for a joke and then backing out. I don't want to put pressure on you but even though we've talked about this a lot, I'm not sure you really understand what's involved. This isn't just some two-week glamour vacation where you get spanked by cute guys and play little sex games."

Marissa stared at him, a little disconcerted. Had he peeked into her head? She licked her lips and said, "Tom, I know how important this is to you. I have to be honest, I'm not really sure what it's all about, but I'm certainly willing to go in and listen. I know you want me to do this thing and I want to do it for you. I won't let you down, I promise."

The valet opened Marissa's door and she let him take her hand to help her out. If he was any indication, this place was packed with gorgeous guys! A little young for her taste, but definitely built. She followed Tom through the big doors where they were greeted by a tall, older woman with great cheekbones.

She kissed Tom on both cheeks European style and said in a rich, French accent, "Tom, *cher*! Welcome. And this, oh!" The woman took Marissa's hands into her own and said, "You, lovely girl, must be Marissa. Welcome, dear. We are so pleased to have you."

Marissa smiled, warming to this kind woman with her gray eyes graced with smile lines, her grip cool as she held Marissa's hands. She stepped back and said, "I am called Claudette. Come, Michael is waiting."

Tom and Marissa followed Claudette, Marissa making note of the older woman's bare feet. She looked at Tom to see if he had noticed, but if he had, he didn't seem to find it unusual. Passing through the elegant entry hall, they entered a large study where a barrel-chested man behind a desk was waiting for them.

Rising, he said, "Hello, Mr. Reed. A pleasure to see you again. This must be Marissa. Nice to meet you. I am Michael Coddington." Marissa took his offered hand. He resumed his position behind the desk as Marissa and Tom took the large yellow leather seats in front of it.

"I presume Tom has explained what we are about, Marissa?" As she nodded, he continued. "I have the contract here for you to sign, but only after you hear all that I have to say and are certain this is what you want to do."

Marissa swallowed nervously. This wasn't quite so carefree and daring as it had felt a few minutes earlier in the car. She felt Tom's hand reassuringly squeeze her own and she managed a small smile.

Michael sat back and surveyed the young couple sitting in front of him. Tom looked anxious, like an overeager puppy waiting for his bone. Marissa looked anxious as well, but anxiety of a different kind. She masked it rather well, and her face was set in a calm smile, though nervous fingers twisted a rather lovely sapphire ring on her right hand.

"Marissa," he said, deciding to be direct. "Are you ready to come to us? Are you ready to give two weeks of your life to becoming the submissive slave girl Tom wants you to be?"

Marissa nodded, her eyes wide, expression serious, her hands still twisting slightly in her lap. Michael's smile was warm as he said soothingly, "Please, relax. This isn't a life sentence you're coming to! You may even find you enjoy it. It will certainly be a challenge, and you look like a woman used to facing challenges."

Marissa sat up slightly as he said this, looking more resolute. She *was* a woman who faced challenges. She was Marissa Winston, damn it, and she always got what she wanted, and right now she wanted Tom. If this was the way to get him, bring it on!

Michael nodded slowly, as if she had spoken out loud and continued. "The next two weeks will be something of a revelation for you, Marissa. I know you may believe at this moment you are submissive, and that you want to be trained to serve Tom Reed as his lover and his slave."

Marissa glanced toward Tom, wondering if he believed this, not sure herself if she did. But Tom was looking at Michael and she turned back to face him as well as he said, "We will help you to test that resolve, to delve into parts of yourself you may have never examined. This isn't a game." *Yeah, yeah, I've heard this before*, Marissa thought, annoyed. "If you agree to the terms in the contract, you'll be getting a chance very few people have. It's the chance to really explore your inner self, not only your submissive nature, but your whole concept of yourself as a sensual being.

"We've discussed this at some length, you and I," Michael said, now turning to Tom. "But it's important we discuss it again, and make sure Marissa has a good understanding as well." He paused for effect, looking slowly first at Tom then at Marissa. She wanted to scream at him to cut out the melodramatics, but she also felt she had better hear what he had to say, so she sat silently, trying to look calm and serene. Her hand rose to cover the small pulsing at the base of her throat that always happened when she was nervous.

"Big picture," Michael continued, "is that for the two weeks Marissa is here, she will belong completely to us. Marissa, if you sign that contract, you give up all rights, except, of course, the right to terminate the contract and leave the program. But if you stay in it, you are in fact and in deed our property, to use and to train as we see fit. That means you don't decide when you get up or go to sleep.

We do. You don't decide when you eat or even *if* you eat. We do. You don't decide what clothing to wear or even if you wear any. We do. If you disobey and we decide you should be punished, we choose the punishment and execute it, and we decide when you've had enough. You don't decide who will use you sexually, who will whip you, how they'll whip you, when they'll stop or if they'll stop. We do."

Marissa sat very straight, biting her rather luscious lips as a slight flush crept up her cheeks. What he was saying frightened her, and yet deeply excited her at the same time. Much of the fight, the games with which she tried to manipulate Tom to "claim" her, to "force" her, were still unexamined in her psyche. She had never really delved into why the fight turned her on so, or what motivation made her crave the rough sex and subsequent loss of self. She had just sought out the experience, and had greedily taken what she could get.

And now this burly man was blithely and calmly describing how she would be controlled, used and possibly tortured, all in the name of "training" her for her rich lover who would come at the end to claim his remodeled prize. It was definitely a game, but what a delicious one! Marissa crossed her legs, feeling a sweet heat inside her that made her glad she wasn't a man so there was no evidence of the arousal his words were causing.

But Michael was an observant man and he saw the flush, the shifting position, and the overbright eyes and knew a slut when he saw one. This one was going to be easy. Easy to use, but how easy to mold? Her mettle was untested as yet, and she had a long way to go.

Turning his attention to Tom he said, "Mr. Reed, are you comfortable with what I've been telling Marissa? I know we've discussed it before, but now that she's actually here and it's no longer an intellectual exercise, do you still feel this is something you want? I completely understand if you do not, I assure you. Your deposit will be refunded and we will remain friends."

"I want it, if Marissa does," Tom affirmed, looking rather grim but resolute.

Michael nodded and continued. "One thing we haven't really emphasized is the fact you are to have no contact whatsoever with Marissa during these two weeks. You may call me at any time but she is to be left undisturbed. It would negatively affect her training if—"

Both Tom and Marissa interrupted, with Tom saying, "No contact? But I was going to—" while Marissa blurted, "Tom gave me my own cell phone! I'm to call every night!"

"Stop, both of you," Michael said, his voice a command, and they did. "If you'll stop to think a minute, I'm sure you'll realize how detrimental that sort of contact would be. As I've said over and over, this isn't a game. Think of it as boot camp for submissives, if you will. If Marissa knows she can call you at the drop of a hat, every time something happens that makes her nervous or uncomfortable, she isn't going to, shall we say, properly apply herself to the task at hand." Tom started to speak again but Michael held up a beefy hand and said, "No. Hear me out. This is essential, and if you cannot abide by it, we'll shake hands and no hard feelings and nice to have met you. But if she stays, she stays on our terms. And that means no direct contact. Period."

Turning to the young woman Michael said, "Let me ask you something, Marissa. Why are you here? What do you want from this experience?"

"What?" Marissa's voice cracked a little and she cleared her throat and said, "Excuse me?"

"I'm asking, dear, what you are doing sitting in that chair. Are you here just because Tom wants you to be here, and you'd do anything to please him, to 'hang onto your man' as they say in the country songs?"

Yes, that is exactly why I'm here, she said silently. To hang onto him and his lovely penthouse, and the fantastic sex and that fresh-squeezed orange juice in the morning and the new lovely emerald earrings and sapphire ring!

"Or," continued Michael who luckily for her could not read minds, "do you want to learn what it is to truly submit? To submit in the face of difficulty, to do things that might not match your idea of yourself as the gorgeous, sexy lover and constant center of attention?" Marissa bristled slightly at this description, though were she honest, it was an accurate one. She was hot and she knew it.

"I'm asking because I really want to know. It isn't a requirement that you wish to submit in order to do so, but it will make your experience so much easier, so much more worthwhile, if you examine your own motives and know why you're here. It would also be more honest for Tom, for your lover who wants you to be his submissive and loving slave girl."

Both men looked at Marissa now and she resented this scrutiny, but figured it came with the territory. Dutifully she gave the answer she felt was expected. "I want to learn to submit with grace for my lover, for you, Tom." Marissa ducked her head, looking submissively at Tom through long lashes as she continued. "I want to learn to be a slave girl who will satisfy his dominant needs and my own submissive ones."

Tom looked enormously pleased, but Michael only narrowed his eyes at her, his face impassive. He'd seen her type before, many times. But they would strip that submissive façade and find out what she was really made of, make no mistake about it. In the meantime he said, "Then I need you to be willing to trust me and my staff. We know what we're doing, and I hope you've both learned enough about what we do to believe that. So, no contact, agreed, Mr. Reed?"

"Agreed." Marissa's eyes slid over to his, but she didn't protest.

"Good." Michael nodded, pleased with this small but essential victory. "Marissa, hand your purse to Tom. You won't be needing it here."

"My purse! I've got things I need in there! You can't take a woman's purse!"

"I can take anything I want, and the sooner you realize that, the better off you'll be, young lady." His voice was stern now, the patience wearing thin. Reluctantly Marissa handed her purse to Tom who took it, holding it awkwardly in his lap for a moment before setting it next to his chair on the floor.

"Now then," Michael said. "The contract." Michael passed a copy to each of them. It was printed on heavy bond paper of pale blue. They both began to read.

Slave Contract between Tom Reed (Owner), Marissa Winston (slave) and Le Chateau L'Esclave (Trainer), dated —

This contract is provided as a secure and binding agreement which defines in specific terms the relationship and interaction between Marissa Winston, hereafter termed "slave", Tom Reed, hereafter termed "Owner" and all staff currently residing at Le Chateau L'Esclave, hereafter referred to collectively as "Trainer". This agreement is binding. This agreement must be entered voluntarily, but cannot be broken except under the conditions stated herein.

Term –

This contract will be binding for a period of two weeks (fourteen days). At the end of that time period, which will begin on the date of all signatures to this contract, this contract will be terminated.

Slave –

The slave, having received permission from her Owner, agrees to submit completely to the Trainer in all ways. There are no boundaries of place, time or situation in which the slave may willfully refuse to obey the directive of the Trainer without risking punishment. The slave also agrees that, once entered into the Slave Contract, her body belongs to her Trainer, to be used as is seen fit within the guidelines defined herein. The slave agrees to please the Trainer to the best of her ability, in that she now exists solely for the pleasure of said Trainer.

The slave agrees to the use of her body by the Trainer in any manner the Trainer sees fit. This includes all types of sexual interaction, insofar as it will aid in the training of the slave for the Owner. It also includes the right to inflict punishment as described herein.

Trainer –

The Trainer accepts the responsibility of the slave's body and wellbeing, and agrees to care for the slave in all regards for the duration of the contract. The Trainer accepts the commitment to train the slave in the art of submission. The

Trainer will not use the slave in any way that would result in profit to the trainer, including but not restricted to prostitution.

Punishment —

The slave agrees to accept any punishment the Trainer decides to inflict. This includes, but is not necessarily limited to, whipping, cropping, spanking, caning, withholding of food or water, isolation, bondage, verbal and physical humiliation and any punishments specified in advance and agreed to by the Owner and Trainer. Punishment of the slave is subject to certain rules designed to protect the slave from intentional abuse or permanent bodily harm.

Termination of Contract —

This contract may be terminated at any time, by any party. However, should the slave or Owner choose to terminate this contract, the slave will be immediately removed from the premises, and will not be allowed to return under any condition. No refunds will be made to the slave's Owner, even if a substantial portion of the training period remains unused.

The Trainer can withdraw from this contract at any time, should the slave prove "untrainable". In the event the Trainer chooses to withdraw from the contract, a full refund will be made to the Owner, and the slave will be permanently barred from the premises.

Slave's Signature —

I have read and fully understand this contract in its entirety. I accept the Trainer's claim of ownership over my body during the period of this contract. I understand I will be commanded, trained and punished as a slave, and I promise to be true and to obey with grace to the best of my abilities. I understand I cannot withdraw from this contract except as stated in this contract.

Signature:

Owner's Signature —

I have read and fully understand this contract in its entirety. I agree to the terms stated herein, acknowledging that the Trainer will own my slave for the duration of this contract, and I am to have no direct contact with my slave for the duration of said contract. I agree that, if in the event the slave withdraws from this contract at any time, no refund will be forthcoming, and the terms of the contract will become null and void.

Signature:

Trainer's Signature —

For the duration of this contract, I agree to accept this slave as my property, and to train her to submit with grace and passion. I shall provide for her security and wellbeing and command her, train her and punish her as a slave. I understand the responsibility implicit in this arrangement, and agree no harm shall come to the slave as long as she is mine.

Signature:

Michael watched their faces as they read. Tom was reading carefully, pursing his lips slightly, no doubt debating the legal aspects of it in his business brain. Marissa's flush had deepened to a pleasing pink and her lips were slightly parted. She was probably reading the part about being used sexually and it was turning her on. The poor girl had no real idea what was in store for her, if Michael could read women, and he could. He could see by her bearing and by her very real good looks that she was used to getting just exactly what she wanted, at least in the bedroom. Slave training was going to be a rude awakening for this so-called submissive.

It was quite possible she would be thrown out of the program, but Michael, a professional, was determined they would all give it their best effort. He genuinely liked Tom, the little he had gotten to know him. While he wasn't convinced Marissa was "the right one" for him, that wasn't Michael's decision. He would just do the best he could to mold Marissa into the submissive slave Tom seemed so desperately to yearn for.

Tom was finished reading first. He took out an expensive-looking pen and, placing the contract on the polished desk, signed it on the line marked Owner. Michael observed the barely contained excitement in his demeanor. Once done, Tom looked over at Marissa who had also finished reading. With a question on his face, he held out the pen to her.

Marissa took it, her long fingers closing elegantly around it, hoping the slight tremor of nerves didn't show. Michael was leaning back in his seat, his face speculative, almost as if he was daring her not to sign it, to wimp out, grab her purse and run. Well, fuck Michael, and fuck Tom, too. She would sign the damn thing and show them all her *grace*, whatever the hell that was. Without allowing herself to think about the astounding terms laid out in the contract, which essentially took all of her civil and human rights away, Marissa signed on the line marked, "slave", committing herself to something that was to shape her future in ways she never imagined.

Chapter Four

Marissa sat on the bed in the room that was to be hers for the next two weeks. She kept nibbling her nails, a habit she had never quite completely broken, then catching herself with annoyance and stopping. There wasn't even a mirror in this place, for God's sake! How could she check her hair and makeup? Not that she could do anything about it, since they'd taken her purse. After they had signed the contract in duplicate—one for Michael, one for Tom, none for her, naturally, as little miss slave girl—Michael had essentially dismissed Tom. He had seemed a little reluctant to go, which pleased Marissa. He would miss her these two weeks and that would make his heart all the fonder, hopefully.

She was surprised at her own very nervous reaction as Tom left the office, truly leaving her alone. After all, this was just a trumped-up, rather elaborate, and, she was sure, quite expensive game, but a game, nonetheless. There was no such thing as a "slave contract" and it wasn't binding in the least, whether she'd signed it in duplicate or a hundred times over.

Still, Tom was gone and she had no purse, no phone, no identification, nothing that was hers—they'd instructed the valet to leave her luggage in the trunk, as she wouldn't be needing it. She was feeling very vulnerable and young when Claudette entered the office after seeing Tom on his way.

"Ah, *chère*," she said in that charming accent. "I am so glad you are ours now. Let me show you to your room. We'll get a little acquainted before you meet Aaron." Marissa stood, relieved to see another woman, relieved to be getting away from Michael who made her nervous the way he seemed to look inside her head. She followed Claudette out of the study and up the long stairwell to her bedroom.

Claudette had left her for a moment, telling her to sit on the bed and see if it was comfortable for her. She would be right back. When she returned, Claudette was carrying a large duffel bag, which she set on the floor, as there was no furniture in the room but the large bed upon which Marissa sat, looking beautiful and very nervous.

"I brought your equipment, darling. These items are especially for you while you're here. You may strip now." As Claudette bent to unzip the duffel, she seemed to expect Marissa to obey. When she realized Marissa was still sitting on the bed, staring at her, she said, "What's the matter? Didn't you hear me? Get up and strip!" Claudette's voice was markedly more strident than when she had been in the presence of the men. "Aaron will be here soon! You must be naked! Hurry."

"Naked? Now? Here?" Marissa looked confused, as if she couldn't be hearing correctly.

"Why not now and here, you silly girl? You will be naked now at all times, didn't they tell you that?" Michael's words came back to her now… "*You don't decide what clothing to wear or even if you wear any. We do.*" It had sounded so sexy at the time, but now, faced with a middle-aged woman ordering her to strip that was something else again! Despite herself, Marissa watched in fascination as Claudette began to remove items from the duffel bag.

She pulled out long links of thin, fine silver chains, which had clips on either end, like a dog's leash. Next came soft black leather wrist cuffs lined with lamb's wool. She was laying these neatly on the end of the bed as she again admonished, her voice stern, "Marissa. Get up, now. Strip. You don't want to start your stay here with a whipping, do you? That will come in time. For now, let's ease into this, shall we? I promise, it will be so much better for you if you do."

Well, this is what she'd signed up for, wasn't it? She had a good body, nothing to be ashamed of. In fact, it was definitely a selling point. Whoever this Aaron was, he'd probably be drooling all over himself, just like the rest of them when she was finished with him! Holding onto this bravado, Marissa slid down off the high bed and stood, slipping off the pretty little sandals she was wearing and kicking them aside as she reached back to unzip her dress and step out of it.

She hesitated for a moment, standing uncertainly in her pink lacy bra and matching panties until Claudette said, her voice impatient, "Get on with it, girl. Do you think I haven't seen breasts before?"

Chagrined, Marissa unhooked the clasps of her bra and let it slide down her arms. Her breasts were not especially large, but they were beautifully shaped, like lush peaches perched firm and high on her torso, the nipples a pale pink. Her waist was long and tapered, widening at her hips, which were still girlish and were parentheses to her little pubic mound of dark copper-colored curls.

She knew she was lovely and her perfection gave her courage as she stood, wondering what to do with her arms, while the older woman continued to remove items from the bag and place them on the bed. Claudette hadn't even glanced her way, evidently completely indifferent to Marissa's considerable charms. That was fine with Marissa. She wasn't interested in women anyway, and certainly not a middle-aged servant at this trumped-up sex spa!

She couldn't help but stare at the items neatly lined up on the bed. There were the chains and cuffs, and in addition, Claudette laid out a black whip with many strips of supple leather. She laid it so the tresses were smoothed out in long, clean lines. Next to this, she produced a riding crop with a short, thick strip of dark red leather folded over onto itself. Next to that was laid a single lash whip, one long, thin braid of black leather protruding from a short, thick handle. That looked dangerous!

Marissa felt a fascination that was at once horrified and eager. Tom had a flogger at home and he had used it on her, never very hard, but it had been exciting. She loved the idea of being whipped and "forced". Again, it was always the *idea* of it that had intrigued her. Marissa had never really submitted to anything at all but the gentle whippings, especially when he whipped her pussy, "forcing" her to spread her legs for him, had been a majorly serious turn-on. She felt her body tingle with anticipation and again whispered her silent prayer, thanking God she had been born a woman, with no awkward penis poking out to give her away.

When Claudette produced a bright red ball with straps attached, Marissa was genuinely puzzled. "What's that?" she asked, thinking it looked like a huge jacks ball, remembering the ball and jacks game of her childhood.

Claudette looked up at her and smiled, still kneeling on the floor by the duffel. "That's a gag, dear. Haven't you ever seen a ball gag?" When Marissa shook her head, Claudette smiled and said, "Well, you *are* a novice, aren't you, chérie? You will soon become intimately acquainted with that gag, if I know Aaron, and I do."

As she spoke, Claudette stood and smoothed her long, silky gown of a sheer pale green. Marissa couldn't help but see she was naked underneath it, with ample but firm breasts tipped by large, protruding nipples, which broke the smooth line of the silk. Again she looked at Claudette's bare feet and thought about the way she knelt so easily by the duffel.

"Are you a, you know, a slave, too?" Marissa asked.

"Why, of course I am, chérie. I live here. I run the household and control the house slaves. I belong to Michael, who is, between us, rather possessive." She smiled warmly as she spoke, her eyes sparkling merrily. The affection she felt for her master was clear in her expression and Marissa saw the two of them embracing in her mind's eye. She was still young enough to have trouble imagining people over fifty being romantically in love.

Before she could contemplate this further, there was a noise at the door and Claudette hissed, "Kneel! Hurry! On your knees, look down at the floor, back straight, arms behind your back! Move! Aaron's here and he's very exacting!" Frightened by the insistence in her voice, Marissa knelt hurriedly.

"And don't look up, whatever you do! Aaron has very specific ideas about a slave's deportment. Never look above his crotch, unless he tells you to! Or you'll get that first whipping before you know it! And don't speak until spoken to!"

As the doorknob turned, Claudette also dropped to the floor in a graceful curtsey, her pretty gown billowing out around her. Marissa had knelt, feeling awkward and very vulnerable on the bare wooden floor. Claudette's tone had been insistent and Marissa felt the first frisson of real fear.

All thoughts flew out of her head as the door opened on well-oiled hinges and Marissa saw feet clad in expensive-looking dark brown leather boots, coming out of soft, faded denim jeans. She resisted every impulse to look up—Claudette's urgent words still burning in her brain.

"Ah, Claudette. Stand up, sweetheart. You may go." Aaron's voice was deep and rich. Marissa thrilled to the British accent at once. She had always been a sucker for that accent, which wrapped itself smoothly around his strong baritone. He spoke softly, but it was definitely a command rather than a suggestion. Marissa heard rather than saw Claudette rise and leave the room.

Now she was truly alone with this man who so far was only a pair of fine boots and a gorgeous voice. A man standing fully clothed with a naked young woman kneeling at his feet. Marissa felt her throat close, and she was grateful for the moment that all she had to do was kneel and look at the floor. What in God's name had she gotten herself into?

Marissa realized she was tensing her body as she waited for this man to do whatever it was he was going to do. He was standing directly in front of her, a few feet away, so presumably he was looking her over. Unconsciously she sucked in her belly a little, though she had the strong, flat abs exercise and youth still afforded her. Even nervous and afraid, she wanted to look good.

"Stand up. Keep your eyes down. Put your hands behind your head, palms open against your neck." No warm greeting like the other two, no appreciative response to her lovely naked form as Marissa had come to expect from men.

As she stretched a hand to the floor for support he said, "No hands. Stand up gracefully. Push up from the knees and rise like a slave, not some clumsy football player."

Disconcerted, Marissa tried to obey, and while the effect was less fluid and lovely than Claudette achieved, it was a beginning. "Hands on your neck," he reminded her. Marissa realized she was trembling! This was ridiculous! He hadn't done anything to her, he was just telling her to stand up so he could check her out. Check out the merchandise, no doubt, before he "had his way" with her, which she was reasonably sure was his intent.

Marissa willed herself to calm down, to slow her breathing, to ease the little pulse pumping in her neck. She couldn't quite decide if what was happening was incredibly erotic or just plain terrifying. Taking a deep breath, she closed her eyes, waiting. "Open your eyes. Don't close them unless or until I tell you to. Look at the ground." Startled, she opened her eyes and lifted her head a moment, looking right into Aaron's face.

Catching herself, Marissa quickly looked down, but he had been looking right at her, and of course he saw. *Fuck*, she said to herself, *now what?* But curiously he did nothing about it. While she had been busy correcting her mistake and looking down, her body had responded to what she had seen. It was a visceral reaction that occurred in an instant in her brain. She barely had time to register his features—it was more the expression in his eye. Something unyielding but vibrantly sexy, which caught at her and made her gasp as she put her head quickly down. She tried to control her suddenly rapid breathing, annoyed with her own gut reaction to this stranger.

Aaron stood in front of her, watching her struggle to maintain her decorum while standing naked, breasts uplifted by her position, head demurely cast down. Her coppery hair captured the light, making it look almost liquid as it shimmered, red and gold. Definitely her best feature, though those perfect little breasts didn't hurt either. He smiled slightly, secretly pleased she was beautiful. Not that it mattered. He would train whatever was given to him, man or woman, beautiful or ugly. But despite the tight rein he kept on his feelings and emotions when training a slave, his body still responded to a lovely female form.

"Turn around," he said abruptly. "And stay in position. Remember, never fall out of position, no matter what is happening, unless given permission or expressly told to do so. Falling out of position is always grounds for punishment." *Let's see that ass*, he said to himself. As Marissa obeyed, turning slowly, Aaron's smile widened, though he would never have permitted her to see it. Ah! Where nature may have stinted her slightly on her breasts, the ass was perfect. Long, oval globes that indented slightly at the hips, like a well-trained athlete. But the cheeks were full and definitely feminine. A good ass for whipping.

Aaron knew Marissa liked a whipping, or so she thought. She liked what her owner had done with a whip, which passed for a whipping in both their amateur minds. Aaron knew Marissa's background — he'd been part of the extensive discussions with the owner and Michael as they prepared her training program together. It was really just a loose outline. Aaron would refine and adjust it as necessary, based on his observations of the slave girl and on her reactions.

The owner had given permission for Marissa to be used sexually, with no restrictions whatsoever. Aaron felt this was essential for a truly complete training. Not all owners were as generous with their property, and Aaron would never go past what an owner had approved. But this one had said quite bluntly that Marissa was a slut who took what she wanted sexually and only submitted when it suited her desires. He claimed to be happy to see what the chateau had to offer as far as teaching her the finer aspects of sexual submission. He himself had failed he had admitted, looking somewhat miserable, Aaron thought.

For the trainer, the basic game plan was always the same. Break them down and build them up again, in his image. That is, in the image of a properly submissive and passionate slave. Aaron did not create automatons, far from it. He didn't train slaves only to obey and submit. He trained them to burn, to yearn for what their master offered. It was that edge of fire that marked his charges and made his work so sought after by masters and would-be masters all over the world.

When his training was successful, the slave did not need controls or chains, the commitment came from within. It began with a basic tenet. A slave-in-training must yield to another's control in every aspect of their life. Aaron had found that the best way to begin achieving control over another was through the use of restriction. Once the slave began to understand her freedoms are being denied, not because she has disobeyed, but because that is the nature of her station in life, she began to understand the scope of her commitment.

He could see as he admired Marissa's gorgeous body that humility would definitely need to be taught here. And the best way to begin to teach humility was, naturally, through humiliation. He would knock this proud woman down quite a few pegs before he was done and she would be the better for it. He would start now with a small test.

"Marissa. Turn around." Slowly she obeyed. Once facing him she started to look up and, as he saw the uncertainty flash on her face, looked down again. Good. At least she was trying to obey his first directive. "When I speak directly to you, Marissa, you may look at me. In fact, I want you to look at me so I know you are listening."

Slowly she looked up, still keeping her hands behind her head, which also was good. She hadn't assumed that because she could look up she was allowed to drop her arms. Perhaps she had some potential after all. Her arms were probably growing tired now, good.

Aaron began to speak as if he wasn't fully clothed in front of a completely naked woman standing at peculiar attention in front of him. He didn't betray the slightest interest in her body but said, "A quick little guide for you when we communicate. Rule one, speak only when spoken to. Rule two, never say 'no'. You are not free to deny me anything I ask of you, ever. It's that simple. The word 'no' no longer exists in your vocabulary.

"You *may* ask me to stop something, but be careful how you ask. You will address me as 'sir' at all times. Preface your remarks with, 'Sir, may I speak?' and if, and again, only if I give you permission to speak, you may make a request. If that request is that I stop something I am doing or don't begin to do something I am about to do, you had better have an excellent reason as to why.

"Because you are scared, or not ready or are afraid it will hurt, are most definitely *not* acceptable reasons. If something is going to endanger you and I don't seem to be aware of it, or you believe it is going to cause you permanent harm, you may voice your concerns. I will consider those concerns and decide if they have merit or not.

"If I decide they do not, I will continue and you will have no further recourse. Do you understand, girl?"

Marissa's eyes were big, the pupils dilated as she stared at him. She pressed her lips together for a moment, and then managed to whisper, "I think so, sir."

"Very good," he nodded, pleased she had remembered to say "sir". Her expression reminded him of another basic rule he would impart. "Now, you need to learn never to close anything to me or to anyone who acts as your master, which means everyone here for the next two weeks. You are less than a house slave, you are a cunt, pure and simple."

He was pleased but hid it as he watched the slight flush rise up her neck at the use of the word cunt. Her throat was smooth and long, for a moment he fantasized himself kissing it. But there was business at hand and he shook the image away. He noted the slight jutting of the chin, again he marked that she was proud and would have to be humbled.

"Specifically," he went on, "you must never close your hands into a fist, never close your legs and never close your lips. If you must cross your legs when sitting, cross them at the ankles. Use your tongue to remind yourself to keep your lips apart. This is a symbolic gesture on your part, an admission that your body exists to serve and pleasure others, most especially your master, of course, for whom we will be the surrogates during your training. You are symbolically saying you are a vessel. A vessel to be used however we see fit — whenever we see fit. Do you understand?"

Marissa nodded and slowly parted her lips, darting her pink tongue between the lush red lips of her mouth. She was aware of her own power and so was Aaron as his cock grew uncomfortably in his pants. He would punish her for that, though it wasn't her fault.

He moved closer to Marissa who had dropped her eyes to his crotch where his evident erection strained. He could smell the sweet citrusy scent of her shampoo as he heard her slight intake of breath. She arched her back slightly, thrusting her perky nipples toward him, letting her tongue slide across her bottom lip for a second, leaving her lips shiny and still parted. The little slut was clearly preparing for, and expecting, a kiss.

Instead she received a sharp slap to her cheek that knocked her face to the side as she gasped in pain. She stood dumbstruck, mouth agape, hand coming round from behind her head to her burning cheek. Before she could protest, Aaron grabbed her by the hair and pulled her head back, hissing into her ear, "I'm not your lover, Marissa. I've trained women far more beautiful than you. Don't think you're going to seduce anyone here, little one. And if I find you trying, I'll cut off this pretty hair of yours and shave your head. Got it?"

Her eyes bright with unshed tears, Marissa nodded, instinctively covering her breasts with her arms as she hugged herself. "And now we find you out of position, slave. Your first punishment already, after only a few minutes together. My, my."

"Please," Marissa began but Aaron cut her off.

"No! No, I didn't give you permission to speak. Control yourself. Apparently I've been misinformed that you had at least some training! That you consider yourself submissive! That you signed up for training because you want what I can offer you!

"Okay, then, take it! Take what you've asked for, little slut, because your sexy little wiles and protestations won't work here. You're going to get a real whipping, probably for the first time in your life. And you're going to take it and thank me for it. Got it?"

If she was going to balk, to run out, to renege on the contract, this would be the time she did it. And if she was going to do that, Aaron wanted it to happen sooner rather than later. He didn't have time to spend on wannabe sex kittens who thought discipline and submission were just sexy bedroom games.

At present there was a waiting list for his services as trainer, and he'd rather train someone who was worthy of his time. Watching the naked young woman, he would have placed even odds on her running out at this point, if he was a gambling man. He waited for a response and slowly she nodded, though the fast tempo of her breathing and her flushed cheeks and neck showed she was far from calm.

"All right, then. I'm going to teach you a punishment position. You'll be learning a number of positions you will be expected to assume on command. You'll learn their proper names, and you'll practice until you perfect each one and it becomes second nature. When a slave is ordered to assume a position, it should be done quickly, smoothly, gracefully and without question.

"For this position you will need to spread your legs wide apart, bend over at the waist and grasp your ankles. Sometimes you'll be permitted to use the side of a bed, a chair or a table for balance, but today I want full access to your ass. Go on, don't just stand there gaping, bend over and grab your ankles. Now!" Putting his hand on her back, Aaron forced Marissa to bend over. She stumbled forward slightly but managed to grab hold of her ankles without falling over.

It wasn't an easy position to assume without practice, but she appeared to be limber enough to remain bent over with her legs fairly straight and a modicum of grace. Again he grudgingly admitted to himself the girl had potential. And at least she hadn't fled the scene.

He would test her now, see what she was made of, what her motives were. The poor girl was bent and contorted, ass up, hair in her face as Aaron bent down beside her and said, his voice low, "You can't believe you're here, can you? I can see it on your face. You didn't realize what you were getting into, I can see that. But you're here now, aren't you? Do you have the courage, girl? Do you have what it takes to submit? I personally don't think so. I have you pegged as a slutty little wannabe, using some guy's money to have yourself a good old time. Am I right? Don't answer, I wouldn't believe you anyway. I think you're going to get thrown right out of this program before too long. It takes guts, real guts, to submit and I don't think you've got what it takes."

Marissa started to respond, still grasping her ankles, naked and defenseless beside him. "Not a word," he commanded. "If you want to protest, to tell me I'm wrong, prove it by staying in position and taking what I give you.

"But if I'm right and this was all a terrible mistake, this is the time to admit it and get out. Don't waste either of our time, please. Stand up and wait here, and I'll go get your things, call your sugar daddy and you can be back in his penthouse tonight."

To his surprise and, though he wouldn't yet admit it, his pleasure, she remained in position. Whether it was fear of retribution from her owner or a genuine desire to stay and learn something, he couldn't yet say. But there she stayed, bent and waiting, not taking the very clear out he had given her.

"Okay, then. You're staying, at least for now. We'll see how long your resolve lasts. I'm going to use the crop on your ass and thighs. I'm going to whip you twenty-five times and if you fall out of position we'll start over." Aaron walked over to the bed and selected the red riding crop, which was still laid out and waiting.

When he returned to Marissa who was crouched over, ass in the air, legs splayed, his eyes rested on her spread sex, deliciously revealed by her position. Clutching the crop tightly to keep his own hand in check, he resisted his impulse to reach out and grab that luscious sexual fruit. What was getting into him? Usually he easily conquered any sexual desire for his slaves-in-training. They truly became objects to be molded and controlled.

He would focus on the task at hand. He would give this girl the whipping she deserved. Smack—to the ass— so prettily offered up. Smack, again, to the other cheek. Then a thigh, and the other. Marissa jumped and wriggled with each stroke, breathlessly counting each one. She was into it, he could tell. She liked a good cropping. This wasn't punishment, it was pleasure. He was exciting her. If he reached now, right now, to touch that succulent, lovely pussy peeking between those legs, it would be wet.

Well, a punishment shouldn't be pleasurable. A punishment should be a lesson, a reminder that whatever transgression had occurred, shouldn't occur again. He waited a moment, watching her bent, still clutching her ankles, no doubt aware of the highly provocative picture she presented, long, lean legs, body bent at the waist, thick, lush hair falling wildly about her shoulders and face, brushing the ground.

Then he struck, smacking the little pussy between the legs so that Marissa fell out of position, taken completely unaware, squealing in real pain as the sting of the crop against tender flesh registered completely.

"Lie on the floor, slave. Pull your legs up to your body and hold your ankles that way. Keep your little cunt spread and prepare for a whipping. Don't you dare close your legs or it'll go that much worse for you."

Marissa was on her back and she obeyed his command, staring directly into his face, her eyes flashing. The little bitch was still turned on. The smack to her sex had hurt, but the pain had transformed into pleasure, into masochistic arousal. He would soon change that.

"Don't move. You needn't bother to count. I'll stop when I'm ready." Down came the crop, and Marissa screamed, closing her legs. "Open your legs, spread yourself. Now." He spoke quietly with great command, and slowly Marissa obeyed, her eyes wide and pleading.

Once, twice and again, and again, he smacked the tender flesh. Marissa yelped and cried, but she didn't close her legs. Her eyes were squeezed shut and she jerked back at each cropping, as if she could sink into the floor. Aaron struck her breast, letting the little square of leather land smack on her nipple. Marissa screamed again and let go of her ankles to cover the reddening tip of her breast. He smacked the other and her hands flew to protect it of their own accord.

"Please, oh, please, oh, please, stop, stop! You have to stop! I can't! Please! I'm trying to submit, to be brave. It hurts!"

Aaron turned his face to hide the smile that threatened. "Of course it hurts, you silly girl! This is a punishment. This isn't a little sex game like you're used to playing with your boyfriend. You disobey here at Le Chateau and you pay.

"Perhaps now you'll hesitate before being so quick to disregard express commands. You are nothing here, slave girl. All your beauty and your ability to control men is meaningless here. We've seen it all before, over and over. You don't impress us. Now stand up and we'll finish the whipping we started. Assume the position!"

He was lying about one thing and furious with himself because he knew it. Her beauty wasn't meaningless, it was devastating. He hadn't been affected like this for years, and he recognized the danger and knew he must rein himself in tightly or he would fail as her trainer.

Perhaps it was because she was so lovely and thus had forced him to turn his attention to his own shortcomings that she received the swift, hard strikes, which made her scream again and again, begging for mercy that wasn't to be had. Aaron whipped the girl until his arm ached, trying to wipe out the ridiculous desire to throw her down and ravish her on the spot. He left her there, sprawled out of position, a naked and bruised heap on the floor. The lesson had been cut short by his own barely contained desire. He slammed the door behind him.

Chapter Five

Marissa lay still for several minutes, lying tangled where she fell after his final savage blow. Her ass, pussy and thighs were on fire, burning and stinging. Gingerly she reached behind to touch the skin, which was hot to the touch and felt bruised and abraded.

"I can't believe I'm here," she said aloud to the empty room. Slowly she pushed herself up and finally stood on shaky legs, moving toward the high, soft bed. She climbed upon it and collapsed against the soft goose-feather quilt. Even that silky fabric was too rough for her poor bottom and she rolled over to her tummy, trying to get comfortable.

Well, so it was happening. Her first day at the sex spa. But instead of being fucked by Mr. Gorgeous, she had received a rougher whipping than she had ever experienced in any of her BDSM dabblings. She reached back again, touching the hot skin of her ass and thighs, not sure what she thought, how she felt. She had been close, really close, to standing up and saying, "Fuck this, I'm out of here"! But something in his voice, in the open and clear challenge, kept her bent over in that horrible and unattractive position.

Though she'd deny it, Marissa was stubborn as a mule, and when challenged, as he had clearly challenged her, she would go much further than probably was good for her. When he'd made that remark about calling her sugar daddy and getting her things, his voice fairly dripping with contempt, it was all she could do not to stand up and smack him across his smug face. The bastard knew nothing about her! How dare he imply she was a coward and didn't have the courage to submit. The fact he had come very near the truth about her sugar daddy and her expectations of a fun sex-frolic vacation irritated her and made her pause for a moment. For the first time it occurred to her that maybe what she was doing was wrong. Deceitful. Allowing Tom to believe she was more submissive than she was. Trying to mold herself into his object of desire, when it wasn't truly where her heart lay.

She was too wiped out to dwell on these philosophical issues, it was making her head hurt! Her thoughts drifted to Aaron, holding the long, red leather crop in his hand. So calm and off-handedly sexy as he rolled up those heavy linen sleeves, preparing to whip the poor, defenseless slave girl. She felt like a wench caught on a pirate ship in someone's fantasy. Was it hers?

He had whipped her pussy! Marissa had always harbored a secret desire to have her pussy whipped. But the fantasy turned out to be much sexier than the real thing had been. Or at least much less painful! Reality wasn't the sweet, vague sexual suffering of her dreams. It was more of a sharp, stinging pain that felt like a knife across her delicate folds! And yet...and yet it had also been wildly, dangerously erotic. If only it had culminated as it always did in her fantasies, with the punisher dropping down to smooth and kiss the delicate flesh he'd only just beaten. Sighing slightly, Marissa saw Aaron now bending over to kiss her poor, heated pussy but, of course, it was only fantasy.

Her hand dropped lower, between legs she spread slightly for better access, reaching under herself to touch her naked sex. She was soaked! The whipping had really hurt and though she hadn't cried, she had screamed pretty loudly and had begged him to stop as she fell out of position, trying to cover herself with her hands, only to have them sharply rapped with the crop as well.

Toward the end all she had wanted was for it to stop. She had forgotten her initial shame at bending over and splaying her pussy for this stranger, and her own astonishment at herself that she had been willing to do it. With each additional strike of the crop, all thoughts narrowed down into a litany of *stop, stop, please stop* as she struggled alternately to hold her position then giving in to the instinct to protect herself.

With Tom she would moan artfully with each kiss of his lash, making sure her body was displayed to her best advantage. His whip sometimes stung a little, but never to the point she lost her decorum. It did get her very hot and she was always ready to be fucked after the flogging sessions.

Maybe this was just her body's conditioning—so now that she had gotten her first "real" whipping as Aaron had promised, her body was responding by readying itself for the expected pleasure which always followed. But Tom wasn't here. Marissa's thoughts drifted to her lover, to his slim, naked body and his sweet, hard cock, always at the ready for her. What would he think now, seeing her lying there, naked and red-assed? Well, he had bought and paid for this, hadn't he? This is where he wanted her.

What was she doing here? All her life she had entertained the fantasy of submissive slave girl, but it had always been just that—a fantasy. She had gone with the girls to that wild party where she had met Tom and it had been a blast. And the time with Tom had been so exciting and sexy, even if he himself wasn't necessarily her dream man. There was probably no such thing anyway, she mused. But she had truly gotten off on the sex, and she really did love to be tied up and play-tortured and then soundly fucked.

When she had realized how serious Tom was about her behaving submissively, she had readily agreed to this so-called slave castle thing. How hard could it be? And she had signed up thinking she'd get full-time sexual attention with lots of nice whippings and bondage from the sound of it.

Now this Aaron guy was going to train her to be the perfect sex slave. It had sounded fun in theory, but it was finally sinking in that this wouldn't necessarily be a joyride. She was going to have to obey this guy, he didn't seem like someone to be crossed, and she was hardly in a position now to protest. With her butt and thighs smarting, with none of her own things around and Tom probably miles away by now, she was no longer so sure about what she'd signed up for. Was it the right thing? Would she end up wimping out of the contract and make Tom lose whatever money he had put toward this thing? It must have been a ton, judging from the opulence of this place, their big-deal fancy contracts and so-called "expert" trainers.

It was Aaron's comment about submission that came back to her now. About having the guts to submit. She had never really thought about it that way before. In her mind real subs, the ones who lived only to please their "masters" were wimps, pushovers, mindless little empty-headed morons who couldn't think for themselves. While she had planned to put on a show of submission, she certainly never planned to truly submit, not with her heart and soul.

His words, then, had come as a total surprise. The idea it took courage to submit with grace. The implication it was a choice, and even a noble one, to sublimate your own needs and feelings as a gesture of honor and love toward another. The concept was alien but she found herself intrigued. She recalled Claudette suddenly, her serene, lovely face, the look of joy behind her eyes. Claudette who was owned as surely as anyone could be. Was her obvious peace a direct result of her courage and ability to submit? Could she, Marissa, ever learn a grace like that? Did she want to? Could this Aaron really teach her?

Without her bidding, the image in her mind's eye had shifted again from her Tom to Aaron as she recalled the handsome features and the impression of controlled strength. The man was seriously sexy. She probably just needed some time to wrap him around her finger—like Tom, like the rest.

What was his cock like? Tom's was average, she supposed. Not too big, not too little, but just fine to do the job. Aaron was tall, easily six four. Did his cock match the rest of him? She knew from experience one couldn't judge a book—or a man—by his cover. And that stuff about being able to tell by their thumbs or feet was nonsense.

As her thoughts roamed over the possibilities of Aaron's endowment, her fingers found their way again to her very wet pussy. Slowly she began to massage herself, yielding to the lovely feeling of warmth her fingers elicited deep in her belly. She could always get herself off better than any man could. They were usually so wrapped up in their own pleasure anyway. She had faked more orgasms than she could count. Meg Ryan had nothing on Marissa.

She sighed aloud, her mind emptying as she focused on her pussy, arching up slightly for better access. A flash of guilt oozed through her consciousness as she realized it was Aaron motivating her fingers against her sex not Tom. His eyes—were they hazel or pure green? Could she make him have eyes only for her? *Fickle girl*, she laughed to herself before her mind went blank with pleasure and she moaned in satisfaction.

Marissa awoke abruptly to rough hands pulling her up. "What?" she cried out, instantly wide-awake.

"Get up, slut. I can see by your position, with your hands buried in your cunt, just exactly what you were doing before you took your little nap." As Aaron spoke, he flipped Marissa over and took the cuffs still lying on the foot of her bed. Grabbing her slim wrists, he attached first one cuff then the other, using thick, silver clips to close them.

Pulling her arms overhead, he quickly secured her wrists to eyehooks embedded in the headboard for just this purpose. It happened so fast Marissa had no time to react. She started to speak, to protest, to deny but just as suddenly remembered his rule about being silent and clamped her lips together. Then they parted as she remembered his command never to close her lips in his presence.

Aaron saw the conflicting emotions and actions and smiled grimly. "You won't be punished for your obvious slutty behavior, just this one time, only because I hadn't directed you specifically regarding touching this body which no longer belongs to you. I see your owner wasn't exaggerating when he said you were a wanton slut who just took what she wanted and only pretended to be submissive."

Marissa bridled at this remark, visibly angered by it, and Aaron could see it took all her willpower to be silent. In fact, Tom hadn't been quite so blunt, but she couldn't know that. Aaron continued. "So, I can see you aren't ready for the privilege of being left untied when you are alone. Until I am certain you will obey, you're to be tethered to this bed when you're here alone, even when you're sleeping.

"And now, so it's perfectly clear, I'm going to spell out to you what you can and can't do to this body. You may never touch yourself sexually when you are alone, unless for some reason you are ordered to. You will only touch this body, which isn't yours any longer, when I tell you to do so. In fact, you have yet to earn the right to wipe your ass until I tell you that you may. You are a total slut. A nasty little slut who needs to be taken firmly in hand. Do you understand?"

Slowly Marissa nodded.

"Answer me in words, slave. Tell me what you are."

"Please, um, yes, I understand. But about the bathroom?"

Aaron cut her off. "No! I didn't say you could ask a question. I want you to say, 'Yes, sir. I understand. I am a nasty little slut who can't be trusted not to jerk myself off when I am alone'."

Marissa stared at him, her arms pulled taut over her head, wrists firmly secured to the headboard. "Go on, girl. Are you deaf? That's a direct order. Say it!" To punctuate his command, Aaron slapped Marissa's cheek, just hard enough to make the point.

Marissa flushed a dull red, but managed to stammer the words, stuttering over the word "slut". She was clearly offended, but hardly in a position to argue.

"You have far too much pride for a slave, Marissa. I'm getting a measure of you, you know, and you have a long way to go. Frankly, I'm not sure what we can accomplish in only two weeks. Spread your legs."

The transition in his remarks was abrupt, and Marissa didn't process it right away. "Jesus, girl, do I have to repeat everything I say? Do what you're told."

Slowly Marissa parted her long, slim legs. Aaron leaned down and pressed his fingers into her pussy, without warning, without preamble. She gasped at the unexpected invasion. His fingers slid out and up her vulva, deftly finding the little nubbin of her clit. Marissa was barely able to suppress a moan of pleasure, he knew just how to touch a woman. She cried out as his fingers stiffened and he smacked the tender little bud of her pussy.

Instinctively she tried to close her legs, but his bark to keep them open stayed her and she tried to obey. "Show some kind of discipline, slut! Remember, that cunt is mine. Mine to touch and tease if I want, and mine to beat. I'm showing you by hands-on demonstration. If I want to caress," his voice became soft as he again massaged and teased her pussy, using light, feather strokes, lulling her into a sexual reverie, "or if I want to smack!" Again the hard-boned fingers went rigid and smacked her poor little pussy.

Marissa squealed. This was her perfect fantasy, to be tied and played with like this. She was a hairsbreadth away from coming, and her breath came in rasping gasps as Aaron alternately teased and tortured. He saw the flushed features, noted the rapid breathing, felt her engorged pussy lips and knew she was on the edge.

So, of course, he stopped. Standing back, he waited the few moments it took Marissa to realize she wasn't being played with anymore. Her eyes opened and she looked beseechingly at him, sexual need apparent on her face. Forget about keeping her eyes lowered or waiting for whatever was her due. The slut was having fun, and he'd interrupted her fun. It was a game, pure and simple. Such a contrast to Theresa who at this moment was chained to the wall in the dungeon, naked and marked with welts from the caning she had so feared, waiting patiently for Aaron to return and let her down.

Little, shy Theresa didn't even like to be touched sexually. She was submissive to the degree that her own pleasure made her supremely uncomfortable. She didn't feel she deserved physical, sexual pleasure and was keenly embarrassed when Aaron forced her to make herself come or to submit to another's attentions.

But of course Theresa would obey, as she did in all things he commanded, however distasteful or fearful to her. Where Theresa truly longed to submit, and was trying so hard to learn the grace and compliance, this one was a wild child.

At least she didn't have the nerve to beg him to continue, though he could see she wanted to. His own impulse was to strip naked and plunder her perfect little pussy, spread and wet. He wanted to take this bound wench and fuck her 'til she screamed. One of the perks of the job—and there were many—was he got to fuck the merchandise, if he chose.

But in fact, he almost never did so. He took his job seriously, and it was rare a slave-in-training would actually benefit from being fucked by her trainer. In fact, it was usually detrimental as it put them on too even a keel, and made the slave confuse the trainer for a lover. This one clearly was still under the mistaken impression she was here to be pleasured and serviced, as opposed to the other way around. It was his job—and in this case would be his pleasure—to teach her just how mistaken she was. He'd seen "brats" before and she was no different. If she didn't bend, he'd break her.

"Close your legs."

Slowly Marissa obeyed, her dark eyes flashing. Aaron released her wrists from the headboard. "Are you hungry? Thirsty?"

Marissa pressed her legs together, trying to focus on what he was saying, clearly agitated from being pulled back from the edge of orgasm. "Yes, sir," she said, attempting to sound meek.

"And do you need to use the facilities?" He unlocked and removed the cuffs. Looking slightly embarrassed by the question, which was amusing in the circumstances seeing as she was butt-naked and had just been finger-fucked, Marissa nodded and looked away.

"Good. Hold it. It will help you to concentrate. I'm going to teach you a few new positions, which you'll need to work on before you get to eat or drink. I will let you use the bathroom after we go over a few moves. Then once you show me the positions, I'll decide if you get to have dinner or not. Stand up."

Marissa stood as ordered, hugging herself in that familiar protective gesture he'd seen so many times before. Her breathing had returned to normal and he could see she was resigned to the fact she wasn't going to get to come.

"We'll start with some very basic positions. You must learn to respond immediately when I, or anyone in a position of authority over you, calls out the particular position. Failure will result in immediate punishment, so pay attention." As he spoke, Aaron picked up the red leather crop that had marked poor Marissa's bottom so recently. He saw her eyeing it apprehensively and smiled, slapping it lightly against his open palm.

"The first position is called 'attention'. I'll demonstrate. You stand with feet and ankles together, almost touching. Arms at your sides, back straight, eyes open and focused on the horizon. Do not move or shift your gaze. Okay, let's try it. Attention!" Marissa obeyed, looking like an army cadet, except for her naked breasts, which were thrust out in an alluring manner that drew the eye down her slim curves.

"Back straighter, chin up," Aaron barked, though in fact her position was excellent. He walked slowly around her, silently daring her to shift her gaze. Her eyes flickered, but remained staring ahead, though her breasts heaved with her effort to stay still and at attention as his crop slapped against his hand, an implied promise that made her flesh tingle.

After a few moments he said, "Good. The next position is called kneeling up. It's the same as when you stand at attention, as you are now, but you are on your knees. When I give the command, you just go down on your knees. Don't use your hands. Sink down gracefully and stay fully upright, arms at your sides."

As Marissa knelt, her strong legs folding easily beneath her, Aaron looked for something to criticize but could find nothing. He surveyed her for a moment, admiring her thick, wavy hair, her large, dark eyes, her strong chin and delicate throat. Her skin was dewy, almost luminous, pink on pale like the inside of a seashell. He found himself wanting to stroke her and he drew himself up, feeling ridiculous, glad she couldn't see him.

"A common position, and the one you will be in most of the time around me when I'm not using or instructing you, is called kneeling down. You kneel with your knees far apart, resting back on the heels. The back is straight and the hands rest on the thighs, palms up. Keep your chin up but lower your eyes. Go ahead, kneel down."

Marissa settled back on her haunches, trying to obey. "Further apart. Spread your legs further apart. Show me your cunt, slave. Display yourself and demonstrate you are available for use." Marissa flushed again, but slowly spread her knees farther, completely exposing her naked sex.

"Very nice. You have some potential," Aaron admitted, and he thought he detected a ghost of a smile on those luscious lips. "I want you to practice these positions when you're alone, when you're not tied to the bed. And Claudette will work with you when you have your grace lessons. She'll teach you about posture and how to move so you are more pleasing to the eye. And she'll teach you the other positions any trained slave is expected to know. I'll expect you to be proficient at them all over the next few days. Don't waste my time by not responding to a position command or you'll definitely pay the price.

"Now, about that trip to the bathroom. I'm sure you're ready to pee for me now. That's right. Don't look so surprised. Of course you're going to do it in front of me. You're going to do everything in front of me for the next two weeks. You have no privacy. You don't exist as a separate entity unless I say you do. Remember, all parts of your body are now mine and cannot be shielded by natural or false modesty.

"So get up and follow me, slave. Let's see that courage you think you have in action." It was the perfect thing to say as it stopped Marissa from refusing, which she had been seriously considering for a moment. Slowly she stood up and followed the tall man out of her bedroom and down the hall.

It was a smallish bathroom, as was fairly common in these old houses. Aaron pointed to the toilet and said, "Sit." Marissa sat down, realizing as she did so her bladder was really quite full. She hadn't been to the bathroom since before they had left Tom's apartment, many hours ago. And yet she couldn't seem to go, not with this man standing in front of her.

Aaron smiled. He had been expecting this. It was common for his charges to be shy at first about using the toilet, especially when they had to move their bowels. But he had found this was an essential tool for stripping away their misplaced modesty, for bringing it home that their bodies were truly no longer their own. If they held themselves too tightly in control, he would "assist" them with an enema, and then watch their blushing misery as they finally did as he bid them, their bodies betraying their last efforts to avoid complete submission.

"Come on, Marissa," Aaron said, feigning impatience. "It's dinner time. Don't you want to eat? If you don't go now, you won't be going down to supper, that's for sure. You'll stay here in the bathroom until you pee, and then you'll go straight to bed. Think about it. I've already seen all you have to offer. If you think a little piss is going to embarrass me, think again."

Desperation overcame embarrassment as Marissa released her muscles and urine splashed into the bowl. She started to reach for the toilet paper but Aaron stopped her. "No. I'll do it. Put your hands on your head." She obeyed, though her face betrayed her emotions as she squeezed her eyes tightly closed and bit her lips.

"Open your eyes! You forget yourself, and so soon." Aaron's voice was gruff as he fought with his own desire to give in to the poor girl and give her her privacy. What was wrong with him!

Taking a deep breath Marissa opened her eyes, focusing on the wall. Her face was red with embarrassment. "Better," he acknowledged.

Aaron pulled some of the tissue down and knelt between her legs, gently wiping the droplets of urine from her pussy, dropping the soiled paper into the toilet. "Good girl," he said. "That wasn't so bad, was it? Get used to it. I won't always be wiping you, but it's my prerogative if I wish to, and you should know that." Aaron washed his hands in the sink and then said, "Go to your room. A slave will be up shortly to take you to dinner. I'll see you in the morning, if you make it until then."

Chapter Six

Marissa's knees hurt. She was kneeling by a large hand-painted ceramic bowl of fragrant, steaming stew on the ground next to her. She was naked, her hands loosely bound with the long, black velvet leads Scott had put on her when he came to collect her. He had barely said a word to her, announcing only that he was a house slave and had been sent to collect her for dinner.

The other house slaves were sitting at a long table with benches on either side in a room just off the kitchen. They weren't paying much attention to Marissa, at least not directly. Their bowls of stew were on the table in front of them. They were using large silver soupspoons to eat and mopping the delicious broth with fresh-baked bread from their own ovens.

Marissa was starving, but felt ridiculous sitting naked on the floor with no utensils, as if she was a dog, expected to lean over and lap the hot stew. There was a piece of bread next to the bowl. Initially she had protested, but Scott and another slave, Frank, had forced her to stay on the floor, threatening to spank her if she tried to stand again. Humiliated, Marissa sat silently, the delicious food untouched next to her.

The house slaves had been discussing "the new girl", as if she couldn't understand English, as if she wasn't right there near them. "She's pretty, isn't she? Striking even, with all that gorgeous hair." Anne offered this observation.

Anne spoke lightly, but hers was more than a passing interest. When not serving directly as a slave, Anne was the receptionist for the business that was Chateau L'Esclave. Despite herself, knowing it was ridiculous, she had taken more than a slight fancy to the dashing Tom Reed who had brought this girl in to be trained.

When Claudette had ordered Anne to bare herself for him, she had felt almost faint with desire. It was stupid, she was a house slave and beneath his notice, and yet it was he she found herself fantasizing about alone at night on her cot below stairs, or when she was being whipped or sodomized by Michael as a diversion from his love affair with Claudette.

And clearly she wasn't Tom's type anyway. This Marissa was tall and lithe, with those flashing dark eyes and mounds of beautiful, tawny, wavy hair. Anne was petite, barely five foot, with buttermilk blonde hair and pale skin. She could fade into any background. She was the quintessential servant. One barely knew she was there unless she was needed. Mr. Reed had seen her naked and he had looked away, embarrassed. She was a fool to even use him in her dreams. Marissa surely would never let him go.

Still, it wasn't Marissa's fault she was gorgeous, and right now she looked rather pathetic. She looked afraid and lost there in the corner where each of them had been at the beginning. She looked miserable and was probably hungry, but hadn't taken a bite yet. Anne, whose natural impulse was generous, pushed down her own secret little longings for Marissa's owner and turned toward the poor woman.

"Eat, dear," she said kindly. "You never know when you'll get another chance, especially when you're training.

They can withhold your food, you know. A very effective tool. And really, the stew is delicious. Amy and Scott are excellent chefs."

Marissa looked up at the little waif smiling benignly down on her. "How am I supposed to eat this stuff without a spoon? It's too hot and I'm not going to lap it like some dog!"

"Pride," Frank intoned, looking down his nose at the naked woman on the floor. "Thinks she's too good to eat off the floor like the rest of us have had to. You're a slave-in-training, bitch. Get over yourself. You're obviously down there for a reason. Don't question your masters, do what you're told. Be glad you're here getting to eat. Your mate-in-training Theresa is shackled in the dungeon right now. She won't be let down 'til bedtime. Maybe I should let Aaron know what a little brat you're being right now. I bet Theresa could use the company."

"Ignore him, he's a bully," Anne advised in a soft voice, scooting closer down the bench to be nearer to Marissa. Louder she said, "Use your bread. Use it as a scoop. And you can lift the bowl and drink from it. They didn't say you couldn't use your hands. You're not being punished. This is just how it starts out. We all had to eat off the floor at first. It teaches humility."

Frank snorted and turned back to Amy with whom he'd been discoursing about the new whips he'd been designing for André. Frank was a tall, well-built man, wearing black suede pants that were cut closely to reveal his thickly muscled legs and ample endowment. His hair was thick and brown, falling in loose curls to just below his ears. He was shirtless and his chest was bare and tanned, and looked recently oiled. Except for the sneer on his face, and a nose that was rather too long, he was quite handsome, and well aware of it.

Frank belonged to André, and was not only his slave but his lover. While Frank did not sleep below stairs with the other slaves, as André preferred his warm, strong body in his bed, he took his meals with them, and served as a house slave in every other way. Because he slept with his master, he felt superior to the other slaves who were claimed by any and all who wanted them.

Hunger overcoming distaste, Marissa picked up the still-warm bread and bit off a piece. Dipping it into the bowl, she brought up a large chunk of tender meat and a piece of carrot and took a larger bite. It was delicious and she was ravenous.

"Like it?" Amy asked. "New recipe, right, Scott?"

Scott, having just taken a huge bite, answered with his mouth muffled with food, "Harrumph." Amy grinned and said, "It smells like pussy, don't you think? It's the lamb and the combination of spices. I think it's heavenly."

"You think anything to do with pussy is heavenly," Frank said snidely. "She's a total slut, this one," he offered to Marissa. "Pussy, cock, anything to do with sex, Amy's there. That's why she has to wear a chastity belt, right, Amy? Can't keep herself from fucking anything that moves."

Amy grinned, seemingly unperturbed by Frank's remarks. Standing, she lifted her cotton shift and showed Marissa her silver and leather chastity belt, complete with a little silver lock at the front. "I can't even pee without asking Claudette or Michael. But when I'm good, they let me fuck little girls like you, darlin'." Amy was tall, about five foot ten, and built like an Amazon with long, lean lines, heavy, sensuous breasts and narrow hips. Marissa didn't know what to say and so remained silent.

"Still, even with a belt on, I can still have fun, right, Diane?" Diane, next to Amy, nodded and blushed. She was a heavyset girl, bordering on fat, and was at present as naked as Marissa—she was the third slave-in-training at the house. "I like a full-figured girl like this slave here," Amy continued, pinching one of Diane's nipples between a thumb and forefinger. Diane blushed a dark crimson and ducked her head, but didn't resist.

"Diane is a pain slut. And a service slut. But not a sex slut. Can you imagine? She doesn't even *like* sex! Her master sent her here to try and instill some sexual fire in this shy little puppy. And wisely, Michael has given her to me to play with when she isn't being trained by the big guys. I'm trying to teach this blushing flower here about the joys of sex, but it's slow going!" Amy laughed and kissed Diane, making a loud smacking sound on her cheek.

"They think maybe she'll respond better to some sweet girl-girl stuff. And you know me, happy to volunteer! Diane tastes as sweet as honey, with a little spice thrown in. Just my type." She laughed again, looking with real affection at Diane who smiled shyly back at her.

Completing the participants at the table was another woman in her mid to late thirties who was introduced to Marissa as Tara. "Tara was left here by her master. When was that, about six years ago, right, Tara?" Frank asked, but the question was really rhetorical, since he remembered the time well. Tara was the only house slave who had been there almost as long as Frank who would be celebrating his seventh anniversary as house slave at Le Chateau L'Esclave this coming March. He had only been

André's lover for four of those years, the four most wonderful years of his life.

Tara had been "abandoned" by her owner before even completing her course of training. He had brought her for the usual submissive training program, to teach her more grace and humility, but had never come back for her when it was over, nor been reachable during the four-week tenure he'd signed her on for. It was all rather vague, but he was linked somehow with organized crime and was believed either to be somewhere in South America or among the fishes at the bottom of the Hudson River, cement shoes on his feet.

Oddly, Tara hadn't been devastated by his failure to reappear, and if asked, was actually quite relieved to be rid of him. While she had loved him in a way, she was also afraid of him but more afraid to leave him, as he'd always promised her that if she did, he'd hunt her down and bring her back or kill her trying, and she had believed him.

Michael had taken a liking to her and felt sorry for her, and so had offered her a permanent spot on the staff. The life of a house slave was really quite pleasant, if one didn't mind housekeeping along the lines of keeping up a small hotel, and if one didn't mind being used sexually and physically for the pleasure of others. Tara definitely did not mind and considered it the best perk of the job, which also paid rather well, though she never saw the money. It was being saved for her in an account until she was ready to return to "the real world", which she had no intention of doing anytime soon.

Now Tara smiled at Marissa and said, "Welcome to our little world, Marissa. Keep your head down and do what you're told and you might even learn a thing or two!"

The conversation drifted to "normal" things, like the latest produce shipment and the Saturday night play-party Michael had planned for them. No one seemed to take anymore notice of Marissa, which suited her. She managed to clean out her bowl and was thinking of asking for seconds, when Amy brought a lovely crème brûlée from the kitchen and even slipped Marissa a spoon while no one else was looking. Whatever else she thought about this place, the food was fantastic!

Later that night, still naked except for the strong velvet ropes, which now secured her wrists and ankles to the bed, Marissa mused over the incredible day she'd just spent. She'd been sent to bed early, after being instructed to help with the clearing up, which she didn't mind since they all pitched in.

Under Tara's watchful eye, which was at least less embarrassing than Aaron's, Marissa had been permitted to use the bathroom and wash up. Aaron did not make another appearance, but she was told to be ready for him first thing in the morning as training would begin in earnest.

Marissa turned on her side, pulling at the ropes, testing them, not daring to actually try and remove them. They had enough give to allow her to move, but her hands were tied too high to allow access to the lower half of her body. She had let Tara tie her to the bedposts, and lock the little locks on her cuffs that would keep her there until someone set her free.

Had she lost her mind? Did she want to leave? Here she lay, willingly it seemed, with her butt still sore from the cropping she'd received, tied down and naked on the bare mattress. The lovely down quilts had been removed from her bed—she would have to "earn" them she was told, which annoyed her. At least the room was comfortably warm.

And yet she felt more alive than she had felt in years, maybe ever. It was like being inside of some wild Gothic romance and she was the captive slave girl in a castle frozen in time. Maybe—the thought occurred to her for the first time—maybe she really could learn something here. She didn't particularly consider herself submissive, but she could still learn about things like "grace" and "how to take a whipping" that they all kept harping on. It would make her more appealing to Tom at any rate, who would then let her stay at his penthouse in the lap of luxury to which she had very quickly accustomed herself.

Tom. She realized she hadn't even thought of him for most of the day. Now, naked and bound to the bed, wishing her hands weren't tethered so she could touch her pussy, she thought instead of Aaron. Thank God, *he* was her trainer and not Michael or André! She loved looking at him, when she could, which was difficult because of his stupid rule about not looking him in the face unless he spoke directly to her and wanted an answer. She thought about his hazel eyes thickly fringed with dark blond lashes, his firm jaw and his full, sensuous mouth. His hair was thick, pulled back in its practical ponytail and she wondered how he'd look with it down. Too feminine? No, Aaron was masculine to his core. She'd like to see *him* naked, she thought to herself, smiling devilishly. *If I could get him naked, he'd belong to me*, she thought, quite sure of her talents when it came to captivating men.

She had spent her day at the mercy of this man who had humiliated and tormented her, and yet she couldn't stop thinking about him, feeling her pussy warm up and swell, aching to touch it. She mused, trying to think what it was about him that attracted her, beside the obvious fact of his good looks and that delicious British accent. There was a quality in him far beyond elegance or even intellect, which drew her — a reserve of emotion as yet unreached that fascinated and challenged her. She would get to this man, this *trainer*, one way or another. If he thought he had another in his series of meek, little, passive slave girls longing to be trained by the "master", he had another think coming. In Marissa Winston, this Aaron had met his match.

Turning on her side, Marissa tried to get more comfortable, tucking her hands under one cheek, wishing again she had a quilt to cover her naked body. The enormity of this bizarre first day caught up suddenly with her and Marissa slid in to sleep too deep for dreams.

The next morning Marissa was awakened by Anne who pulled back the curtains, letting in the weak dawn light. Never an early riser by choice, Marissa opened one eye, saw the girl and turned over, wishing she had at least a sheet to pull over her head. She shivered slightly and mumbled something to the effect she was sleepy and to please go away and come back in two hours.

"Get up, Marissa. And hurry! Aaron will be here in five minutes. He won't be at all pleased to find you asleep in bed! Here, I brought you a hairbrush. Use it quickly and then kneel over there on the floor to wait for Aaron." As she spoke, Anne unlocked the little padlocks that held the velvet ropes in place on Marissa's wrist cuffs. At the mention of Aaron, Marissa came fully awake and sat up, rubbing her wrists once the cuffs were removed.

"I have to pee," she announced.

"You can let Aaron know. You aren't allowed to use the bathroom except in his presence or with his express permission. Didn't he tell you that?" Marissa sighed and began to brush her thick, lovely hair, which was tangled from what must have been a restless night's sleep, though she didn't recall waking at all.

"Your hair is gorgeous. But I bet you hear that all the time," Anne offered, smiling shyly. Marissa nodded. She did hear it all the time and was quite vain about her hair. She looked at Anne now, appraising the yellow-white blonde hair that was hung prettily down her back. It was really quite becoming on the petite woman. She was about to offer a compliment back when Anne said suddenly, her voice urgent, "He's coming! I hear his boots in the hall. Hurry, give me the brush. Get down over there. Kneel up, you know what that is, right? Hurry, kneel up!"

The urgency in her voice got Marissa moving and she quickly slid off the bed and knelt as instructed on the floor, while Anne slipped silently out. She felt her heart pounding in her chest as she tried to kneel properly, back straight, high breasts jutting, chin up, eyes ahead.

Before she had time to worry if her position was correct, Aaron entered the room, dressed again in jeans and another linen shirt, this time of a soft, faded black, opened slightly at the chest to reveal dark blond chest hair that made Marissa want to unbutton each button slowly, until she could push the shirt from those broad shoulders.

"Good morning, Marissa. Sleep well?"

"Yes," Marissa responded, and then belatedly added, "sir."

Aaron nodded. "If you have a better day today than yesterday, I daresay your quilts will be restored to you. But of course, that's up to you. Now, shall we go to the loo?"

Again the heat in her face at the thought of peeing in front of him, but she really did have to go and so she nodded. He was out the door as she stood and followed, biting her lip nervously. Once on the toilet, her body responded more immediately than last time. Then, to her horror, she felt her bowels moving uncontrollably. Oh God, she couldn't do this! It was beyond humiliating. Aware she was speaking out of turn, Marissa pleaded, "Aaron! Please, I have to, um, you know. I have to go. I really need to be alone. Please!"

Aaron stood back, a bemused expression on his face. "No one's stopping you. This is a lesson, think of it as such. There is no place for modesty in your life now, Marissa. There's no going back. I can see you are embarrassed, but that's just too bad. You are a slave, and have no rights and no say about that body. Go ahead, do your business. I'm not going anywhere. It's perfectly natural and nothing I haven't done myself." He smiled gently, knowing this was harder than taking a whipping, much more so as there was no sexual overlay to it for Marissa, though there was for some.

"Show me your grace, slave girl. And as a reward, I'll let you wipe yourself. But be quick about it. We have a busy schedule today."

Her face a dull brick red, Marissa gave in to her body's insistence, defecating in front of Aaron, even passing some gas with a flatulent sound that made her actually gasp in dismay and shame. She was near tears as she hurriedly wiped herself and flushed the toilet, leaping up without permission, to wash her hands and flee from the bathroom and back to her bedroom as fast as she could.

Aaron followed more slowly, giving her just a moment of privacy, curiously moved by her very real shyness in regard to her bodily functions. They would have to spend some time desensitizing her from her extreme modesty in that regard. But for now, to the task at hand. "This morning before breakfast I need to see how skilled you are in the art of oral pleasure. Of course, that's very important for a sex slave. I imagine you have had extensive experience but that doesn't necessarily mean skill."

Ah ha, Marissa thought, grateful to be done with the "loo" and now back on more familiar ground. *Now we come to it*, she smiled inwardly to herself. *The man wants a blowjob, and who more handy than his little "slave girl" to provide it? Now I'll get him. I'll make him mine. The way to any man's heart is through his cock, especially with my mouth wrapped around it!* Marissa couldn't suppress the slight grin as she contemplated what was coming. Obediently she knelt, ready to "service" her lord and master. Thus she was startled when Aaron called out, "Scott. You may come in. And ready yourself for Marissa's lesson."

First confusion then horror registered on Marissa's face as she realized what was happening. Scott came in, looking a little sleep-tousled himself, but willing. He was wearing soft cotton trousers held up with a drawstring, and his chubby torso was bare. At Aaron's instruction, he dropped his pants and stood naked, penis at half-mast. For a short man, his penis was surprisingly large, even when only partially erect.

Scott looked over at Marissa, kneeling nude on the floor, and his penis perked up a bit. He didn't say anything in front of the trainer, but his expression was smug and eager. Short and pudgy, with small, neat facial features, Scott was not Marissa's idea of an attractive man. That "slave contract" didn't say anything about blowing the house staff! She wasn't about to suck off this little jerk! Her face was eloquent with her obvious feelings.

As if reading her mind, Aaron said, "When you signed on, you agreed to allow the use of your body in anyway your trainer sees fit. And I quote, '*This includes all types of sexual interaction, insofar as it will aid in the training of the slave for the Owner*'. Now I suggest you wipe that bratty expression off your face and come kneel in front of this boy and show me your techniques, if you have any."

Marissa obeyed, her color high, her eyes flashing with indignation. "*If you have any*" indeed! She'd make Aaron long to be the one in Scott's place! Settling on her knees in front of the house slave, Marissa gently cupped his hot, heavy balls in one hand. Scott sighed and she felt the balls tighten as he visibly swelled to a complete erection, the thick cock now red, veins distended.

Leaning forward, she softly licked the head of his cock, tasting his soapy saltiness, relieved he seemed to be clean and unblemished. Closing her eyes, she imagined it was her lover there, though the image in her mind's eye wasn't clearly of Tom. Feeling comfortable, certain in her expertise in fellatio, Marissa settled down to her task, deftly sliding her long tongue down the thick shaft, enjoying the smooth heat of it as she tickled and teased him to an even harder state.

Bobbing forward, Marissa opened her mouth and let Scott's cock slide down, back into her throat, willing herself to relax and take him without giving into the natural impulse of her gag reflex. Leaning up, she pressed her breasts against his legs, partially for balance, but mostly to turn him on as he felt her soft body against him.

Scott moaned and moved into her, grabbing her hair in fistfuls and thrusting against her.

"Be still, Scott," Aaron ordered, and he at once dropped his hands to his sides and shuddered as he stifled his own impulse to buck into her willing mouth and throat. As Marissa continued to suckle and caress Scott's cock and balls, Aaron admitted, "Not bad. How about his ass, though? Part of good fellatio is paying attention to the ass as well as the cock. Don't you agree, Scott?"

His eyes closed, his face a study in pure bliss, Scott nodded, pulling back from Marissa so his cock popped out of her mouth. She sat back, confused, not entirely focused on what Aaron had just said. But Scott understood quite well, having enjoyed this particular exercise many times as Aaron's "assistant" in sexual training.

Turning, Scott bent down and grabbed his ankles, much like Marissa had been instructed to do for her whipping, though his legs were spread further. Now Aaron commanded, "Go on, girl. Lick his asshole. Show your complete subservience. Show us what a complete slave-whore you really are."

Marissa sat back, instead of leaning forward to do as ordered. "You can't be serious," she finally said, no trace of subservience in her tone.

Aaron's face clouded, his expression dark. "Never more so," he said quietly, daring her to continue to defy him. Scott remained bent at the waist, his little ass offered to the unwilling slave girl, cock straight out at attention. "Spread his cheeks and lick his asshole. I want to see your tongue rimming the hole. And then I want you to stick it in and fuck him with your tongue. Show me what you've got, girl. And then you'll get the beating you deserve for your impertinence."

She sat rigid, the slow, hot color burning up her cheeks. Finally she said, "I can't."

"What? Of course you can."

"No. I could never do that. Lick a man's asshole. That's disgusting! It's unsanitary."

In a second Aaron was by her side. Grabbing her by the hair, he pulled her roughly to her feet. "How dare you! You pretend to be submissive, but you're nothing but a masochistic slut! Doing what pleases *you*, what you think impresses others, thinking you're so bloody sexy you can get away with it! Well, this is what submissive is! You do what you're told, not because it makes you look sexy and appealing, but because your master tells you to do it!" Aaron's normally quiet, controlled voice was loud, his anger evident.

"If your master tells you to lick someone's ass, you do it! You don't question him about how bloody clean it is! Who the fuck are you, missy? The bloody queen of England? My God, we have a long way to go!" Still holding the poor woman by the hair, Aaron made a visible effort to calm himself, breathing in deeply for a moment, his expression easing. In his normal dignified tone he said, "Scott, sit down. This will take a few minutes."

Scott came out of his bent-over position, pants still down around his ankles and sat back against a wall to watch the fun. Aaron dragged a struggling Marissa to the bed and flipped her across his knee as if she weighed no more than a child.

His palm open and slightly cupped, he began to swat her bottom, the sound cracking in the air as flesh met flesh. He was hitting her hard. Marissa struggled and cried, but he held her firm, quickly turning her cheeks a bright red.

As she stilled, exhausted from fighting against his strong grip, Aaron's anger suddenly vanished.

He realized part of his anger was at himself, at his own desire to be in Scott's position. To be the one whose penis was kissed and teased so expertly by this woman with such obvious skill and pleasure in her task. God, he wanted her, and that just wouldn't do! To disguise his feelings, even from himself, he had allowed himself to get angry over what he really should have expected from a novice trainee. Marissa wasn't the first person to balk when being told to perform such an intimate and debasing act, and she certainly wouldn't be the last.

Smoothing the hot, round cheeks of her ass now, Aaron murmured, "Marissa. You have no choice about obeying. You will lick Scott's asshole, if I have to hold your mouth open and force your tongue." Marissa lay still, whimpering quietly against his thigh. "You do have a choice about how you conduct yourself. Do it with grace or do it without. Either way, you will do it. The sooner you accept your circumstance, the sooner you will begin to learn some submissive grace."

Would she leave now? Marissa was probably the least submissive slave he'd ever been charged with training. Unlike Theresa and Diane who had things to learn but were truly submissive, Marissa seemed to fight him at every turn. He considered for a moment telling her to get out. Then the chateau would have to refund the money, which was considerable. But no, that wasn't the reason he didn't dismiss her outright. The truth was, he didn't want her to go. He wanted to savor each day he had with her. What was happening to him? This wasn't merely foolish, it was dangerous.

Pushing his own unacceptable thoughts away, Aaron lifted Marissa from his lap and stood her on her feet. "Are you ready to try this again?" Seeing her face, tear-streaked and pathetic, Aaron resisted his impulse to take her into his arms and comfort her. Instead he said, "Scott. Assume the position."

Obediently, Scott bent over again and Aaron led Marissa to him, pressing her to her knees. He guided her head to Scott's ass, which was in fact quite clean, and waited. She could have gotten up then and left the room, and never come back. Aaron realized he was holding his breath. But instead of bolting, she leaned forward, gingerly touching Scott's butt cheeks, carefully spreading them to reveal the puckered little hole between.

Screwing her eyes closed, wrinkling her nose, Marissa darted out her tongue and licked the tight little opening. Aaron suppressed a smile at her obvious distaste. She was such an innocent! "Go on," he encouraged softly, and Marissa obeyed, pressing her tongue against the sphincter, forcing her way past it a fraction of an inch, her eyes still squeezed shut. Scott moaned with obvious pleasure.

Aaron noted the closed eyes and smiled a little. He would let her get away with it—this time. After a few moments he said, "That was fine. Not so bad, eh? You are very silly about things to do with bottoms, Marissa. You realize we'll have to focus on that, don't you? No point in working on what you're already good at. But this ridiculous shyness has got to be dealt with." He turned from the relieved girl who was wiping her mouth against her hand, her face averted from Scott's still-offered ass.

"Scott. Stand up. Pull up your pants. You're dismissed." Scott quickly obeyed, bowing slightly toward the trainer, and if he felt cheated out of coming down that lovely throat, he certainly didn't indicate it to the trainer.

Aaron led Marissa to the bathroom again, where he turned on the water, letting the steam fill the room. "You'll find shampoo and soap, toothpaste and a brush, and all you need in the shower stall. You may clean yourself up and dry off. You may put on the dress I leave for you on the hook and go down to breakfast. Claudette will come for you for positions training. I'll see you this afternoon."

Chapter Seven

Marissa was just finishing her warm blueberry muffin and coffee, relieved the lateness of her arrival meant she was eating alone. All through her shower she dreaded the thought of eating with Scott and the rest of them, possibly being humiliated by having to hear him give a detailed description of the morning's events.

She had even been permitted to sit at the table, and was allowed a little cotton dress, for which she was grateful. It was a simple white shift, cut close and actually quite flatteringly against the body and so sheer as to be almost see-through. Her nipples were dark against the fabric, and it was clear that she was naked beneath it but still it was something. Her wet hair, looking bronze against the light, was tucked back behind her ears, and her face, devoid of makeup, was honey fair.

Claudette appeared and said brightly, "Hello, *chère.* Difficult morning, I hear." Marissa blushed, turning away.

"Well, you aren't the first to resist that particular exercise, dear. But hopefully one day you will come to realize it is so natural. To worship each part of your master's body is essential. It is not only in homage to him, but a testament to your position as his object and slave. It is not demeaning, though I can see where you would find it so, and some masters would also find it so and enjoy debasing you to prove it. But to me, it is exalting. Yes, that is the word. Exalting to be able to worship my master with every fiber of my being, embracing every part of him as worthy of my love and devotion." Claudette looked up at the ceiling as if the image of her darling Michael was imprinted there.

Marissa looked skeptical and Claudette returned her gaze to the young woman, smiling indulgently. "When you fall in love, dear, you will see. You will see." Marissa startled, surprised Claudette assumed she wasn't in love. Wasn't she? The can of worms that question opened was overwhelming and Marissa decided to ignore it for now. Instead, she obediently followed Claudette to the training room, the same room where Tom had witnessed Theresa being caned while bent over the exercise bar.

"Take off that thing, *chère*. I'll need to see your positions. It's very important for you to learn these positions and then your master need only call out the name of one of them, and you will instantly know what he wants. The positions we teach are standards in the trade. You've already learned a few of them. Can you remember what they are?"

Marissa, stripping off her dress, was surprised at how quickly she had gotten used to being naked in front of people who weren't her lovers or even friends! It seemed so natural here, and everyone was so matter-of-fact about it. At least she was confident about her looks. It must be much harder for someone like Diane, she thought, who was heavy and not especially pretty. But Claudette had asked her something. The names of those positions. She remembered. "Attention, kneeling up and kneeling down."

"Eh, *bien*," Claudette concurred. "And you will demonstrate each one, please?" Marissa did as asked, first standing up straight as a soldier, eyes on the horizon, shoulders back. Slowly she sank to the ground, trying to be as graceful as Claudette was in her movements. Finally she sat back on her heels, spreading her legs, hands on her thighs, palms up.

"Very nice. Did you take dance, ballet?" As Marissa nodded, Claudette smiled.

"All young girls should take dance, and most especially those of us lucky enough to be submissive. Grace is essential. It is not only something of the body but of the mind. Some of these positions I'm going to show you may seem less than graceful, but that is only if you forget to apply your own grace to them. It is your duty as a slave, as an owned and cherished slave, to imbue every act, even the most debasing, with your own natural grace."

Marissa looked at her somewhat blankly. The words were pretty, but she didn't really understand them. Claudette went on. "First, there is what Michael calls the 'pony'. This is an excellent position for a slave who is exhibiting too much pride. It is a lesson in humility. I shall demonstrate." Completely unselfconsciously, Claudette stripped off her own silk gown, which was a deep blue that brought out the silver sheen of her upswept hair and arched eyebrows. She stood completely at ease in front of the younger woman as if it was the most natural thing in the world.

As she spoke, she demonstrated with surprising agility. "You stand like this, feet wide apart then bend at the waist and place the hands far in front of you on the floor." Claudette bent, easily touching the floor while keeping her legs perfectly straight. "The slave should be able to move in this position, walking on all fours and keeping the legs spread apart. This is, as I said, a 'punishment' position, used to bring the slave down a peg or two. Hopefully you won't be called upon too often to assume it. There, now you try it."

Claudette stood and watched while Marissa tried to imitate her, leaning forward somewhat awkwardly at first, and then walking like a crab across the floor, feeling ridiculous. "Not bad," Claudette finally said, and allowed her to stand. "We'll work on it.

"Next, we move from the pony position to a 'graze' position. When you are being punished and treated as an animal, a little pony, *oui*? Well, then sometimes your master will have you eat that way, you see? You will be asked to assume this position when you are already in the pony pose. You are then allowed to drop to your knees, still keeping your legs open wide." Slowly Claudette lowered herself to the ground, her trimly shaved pussy completely exposed.

"In this way," she continued, "you can lower your head to a food dish on the floor by bending your elbows. As I say, this is used as punishment, as eating from the floor or from a bowl on the floor is a good lesson for a disobedient slave."

Marissa tried to imitate the older woman's movement, finally getting it after several tries. She felt ridiculous but Claudette was so matter-of-fact about it all. "These next ones are more for sexual use, as opposed to humiliation. These are poses you will assume to make yourself more accessible to your master, without him having to spell out for you how you should position yourself.

"The first one I'll show you is called 'present'. You present yourself to your master, like so." Claudette knelt, facing away from Marissa, bending forward and lowering her face to the floor. "Sometimes it will be the floor and, of course, sometimes the bed. The back should be arched and the shoulders pressed down. The derriere should be lifted toward the ceiling, the legs spread and the pussy and derriere exposed as you wait for use. The slave can also reach behind and use the hands to further open that area." Claudette did not demonstrate this last direction to Marissa's relief.

Slowly Claudette rose from the position and sat back in a kneel-down position, adding, "The slave is sometimes left in the 'present' position for a lengthy period. This creates a sense of vulnerability, which is appropriate, given your station. You should never *expect* to be used sexually. Each time it is offered, it is a precious gift from your master to you, never to be taken for granted."

While Marissa was musing if this woman was for real, Claudette went on. "The next position is called 'supine present'." She lay back on the floor, and said, "This is to expose the sexual orifices. You lie on the back, hands at the ankles, and draw the legs up as far as possible. Eyes should be on the ceiling." Marissa recalled with aching vividness how Aaron had only yesterday forced her to that position, cropping her poor pussy! She felt a tingling deep in her belly and pressed her thighs together, pushing the image away.

Claudette had Marissa practice these positions over and over, until her knees were aching and muscles screaming. Claudette would demonstrate first, making it seem effortless despite her mature years. Disregarding the awkwardness of some of the moves and the fact she was completely exposing her most private parts, Claudette didn't seem in the slightest self-conscious, unlike Marissa who blushed repeatedly. Claudette showed her other positions as well, including 'oral present', where the slave is on hands and knees, knees apart, torso lifted, back arched, chin up and mouth opened wide. The reason for this position was evident. She drilled Marissa as to the names of each position, finally calling out a position name and expecting Marissa to hop to, which she tried to do and eventually did successfully each time.

Finally Claudette showed her the "inspection position". "From time to time you will be inspected to make sure you are complying with whatever standing orders you have regarding hygiene and appearance. When your trainer or master calls for inspection, you will do the following—first stand at attention. Go on, do it now. I'm going to inspect you and you had better be still and obey, because right now I have all the authority of a trainer over you."

Marissa stood at attention, suddenly feeling nervous, sure this didn't portend well. But Claudette, still speaking in her soft, heavily accented tone said, "*Bien*, now move the feet to open the legs wide apart, lacing your fingers behind the head and dropping the mouth open. Go on, open your mouth and stay perfectly still."

Claudette had put her own gown back on, emphasizing for the moment she was in charge of the still naked girl standing at attention before her. First she looked into Marissa's mouth, actually running a finger along Marissa's gums. Marissa resisted a sudden impulse to bite down as she struggled to stay still, eyes straight ahead.

Satisfied, Claudette slowly ran her hands along Marissa's legs and underarms, tickling her slightly by accident. When Marissa squirmed, Claudette ordered her to stay still and quiet. "I see you shaved this morning, that's good. You should shave twice a day, you must never ever be the slightest bit, how do you say, 'nubby' for your master or whoever he gives you to. That is a serious offense, as it shows lack of respect for your master's property."

Dropping a hand lightly onto Marissa's pubic mound, she said, "You need to trim that pussy, girl." Marissa bristled, sucking in air through her nostrils, her lips a tight line of control. Claudette seemed unaware of her difficulty in having another woman touch her 'there'. She continued. "We'll go get scissors and a razor after this. Doesn't do to have a raggedy *con*, *chère*." Though Claudette used the French slang for "pussy", Marissa knew what she meant.

If she was aware of Marissa's indignation at being assessed thus, she didn't let on. Instead she continued with the lesson. "Next, the slave removes her hands from the back of the head and offers them for inspection." Gently she took Marissa's hands in her own, examining the nails, several of which were slightly chewed and in need of attention. Tsking with disapproval, she lectured about keeping one's nails even and well-kept.

"Finally, you turn away from the inspector and resume a position of attention, lifting one foot at a time for the inspection of feet and toenails."

"Please," Marissa finally burst out, exhausted and thoroughly affronted by Claudette's criticisms. "This is ridiculous. I feel like I'm in some kind of weird army."

"You may indeed feel that way. Though you do not behave with the discipline of even a basic cadet, I must say. You are disgraceful. I shall report to Aaron who will see you are punished for this outburst." Claudette spoke very calmly, but there were two bright spots of pink, one on either cheek. She was not used to being addressed so impertinently by the slaves, most of whom treated her as if she was a master and trainer, even though in fact she was herself a slave.

"Now," she went on quietly. "If you are through with your outburst, we will finish the inspection exercise. On my cue, you will spread your legs, bend at the waist, reach behind and hold open your bottom and pussy."

After the morning's debacle with Scott, and this exhausting morning of holding uncomfortable and humiliating positions, this was simply the last straw. Instead of obeying, Marissa stood up and said, "I'm sorry, Claudette. This is just too much. This slave shit may be what you live for, but I can't deal with it. I am not going to spread my ass cheeks and pussy for you. Period."

Claudette stood back, appraising her. "Are you saying you are leaving? You are out of the program? We should call your owner to collect you? You are admitting defeat, failure? Over something so simple as this small act of submission?"

Marissa paused, imagining the scenario in her mind's eye. It would be a relief to get out of here, away from these crazy sadists and masochists who acted like this was all such a big fucking deal. Tom would come get her and take her home. Home to what? She knew how much he was depending on this whole experience being some major changing force in their lives. He'd sent her here to "teach her to submit with grace and humility". She certainly wasn't doing that, was she? She had yet to submit to a single thing, really, without being forced to do so via someone else's physical strength or threat of a whipping.

And there was Claudette, the essence of grace and serenity, who was able to submit to the most debasing demands with a sweet ease that took Marissa's breath away. Did she storm out and call a man who might now reject her, send her packing, back to her noisy, cheap apartment and her dead-end life?

And Aaron. Her heart caught a moment as she realized that by leaving, not only was she risking everything with Tom but she wouldn't see Aaron again. Ever. She realized Claudette had said something she had missed.

"Well, answer me? What is it to be, girl?"

Face burning, not sure what she was doing or why, Marissa answered by bending over and spreading her own ass cheeks and pussy for Claudette's precise inspection. Whatever game was being played, Marissa wasn't ready yet to throw in the towel.

That afternoon found Marissa waiting in the punishment position — bent over, grabbing her ankles, legs slightly bent at the knees. While the other slaves went to lunch, Marissa was informed she would be spending her lunchtime contemplating her disgraceful behavior of the morning, waiting for her trainer to come and punish her.

More fingernails were nibbled and ripped as Marissa did indeed contemplate what was surely coming. Claudette would have told Aaron all about her refusal to comply, and he would be coming in here to whip or spank her.

At first Claudette left her sitting on the floor, telling her not even to get on the bed. She didn't deserve anything but the floor. After a little while, which Marissa spent staring out the window and wondering for the thousandth time what she was doing there, Claudette opened the door and told her to assume the "punishment position".

Now Marissa shifted slightly, the blood rushing to her head, hoping he'd come soon and get it over with so she could stand up! It had been at least ten minutes, which was a long time to hold such a position, no matter how limber. The door opened and Marissa stiffened, hearing the soft tread of someone entering the room. Aaron had arrived at last, at least the terrible anxiety of waiting was over. She'd take her punishment and get on with it. Maybe they'd let her eat lunch afterward as she was starving!

Marissa grunted and fell forward as a thick leather strap made sharp and sudden contact with her ass. "Get back in position!" A stunned Marissa struggled to obey, her ass smarting terribly from the unexpected blow.

She realized as she hurried to grab her ankles again that the voice was not Aaron's, but Michael's. She hadn't seen Michael since she had signed the contract what seemed like years ago, but was in fact only yesterday. Why was he here, instead of Aaron?

The question flew out of her brain as the strap hit again, even harder. She was pushed forward by the blow but somehow kept her hands on her ankles. "I am going to administer twelve more strokes. You will count them." No preliminaries, no discussion of her errant ways, Michael got right down to business. He hit her again, this time across the tender spot where her thighs met her bottom.

Marissa screamed but managed, "One!" He hit her again and again, the thick leather covering such a large area of flesh at once that it was far more brutal than the heavy flogger which Tom had favored, whose tresses spread the sting so much more gently.

Marissa was yelping and breathing so hard she thought she might pass out in this position, but still somehow she managed to count. Instinctively, she knew Michael was not to be crossed. On the sixth stroke she fell completely out of position and sprawled on the floor.

Grabbing her by the hair, Michael calmly said, "Bad girl. So we begin again," as he forced her to start again at the number one. When he finally left her, her ass a bright, blistering red, her face covered in tears, Marissa fell in a sweating heap, her hair wild about her like some broken lioness, brought down in the wild. She lay where she had fallen, pillowing her face with her arms, too spent to even cry.

Days passed, and Marissa became more accustomed to the routine. She was forced to fellate Scott several more times and to lick his little asshole, which she did, not with pleasure, but at least with obedience. She didn't see Michael again, and tried to make sure she wouldn't by obeying each new command and learning each new lesson as best she could.

Claudette was as calm and lovely as ever, unaware or indifferent to how brutally her loving master had beaten Marissa, whose ass was bruised and marked for several days after. She continued to teach Marissa in matters of deportment and grace, her face a mask of serenity and peace.

But it was Aaron who Marissa waited for, and found herself wanting to please. She freely admitted to herself she had an all-out crush on him and began to plot in her own mind how she could get him to want her, even a little bit. It was enormously frustrating that he seemed so implacable, so indifferent to her considerable charms. She just wasn't used to it!

Today they were going to work on sexual techniques and maybe she would seduce him at last. She realized she had underestimated this man who had trained many other beautiful women and had no doubt had his pick.

"Today we're going to see how much self-control you have, Marissa," Aaron informed her. "A slave shouldn't orgasm until her master tells her to. For some, the pleasure is in watching the slave become aroused but then in controlling her, reminding her through control that the master is in fact the owner of her body, of her orgasm, of her desires.

"It's important for the slave to remain focused on the master, on his pleasures instead of her own. Passion is key. You have already demonstrated reasonable oral technique but a good prostitute can do the same. A love slave needs to show her passion, to prove it again and again while, as I say, always remembering her position as the servant of her master's pleasure. I've found an effective technique for training is for the slave to touch herself while her master's cock is down her throat. You must balance your own passion with your master's pleasure."

Marissa sat very still, not sure what she was hearing. Was he going to let her suck his cock? Mr. Cool and Aloof was going to let her heat him up? She didn't even dare breathe, waiting to see if he called in Scott or Frank, or if it was his own member he was finally going to offer.

Aaron stood in front of Marissa who was kneeling up and said, "Oral present." As he spoke, he unzipped his own pants. She watched, mesmerized, as he slipped the little metal button through the fabric and slid the zipper slowly down. He let his pants fall, and she saw his cock and balls tucked neatly into his black cotton underwear.

Marissa was almost dizzy with desire now—she wanted this man who was training her for another. Dutifully, she got on her hands and knees, mouth opened wide, waiting for his offering, her heart hurtling against her ribs. "Use your teeth," he said, "and take down my underwear. Then slowly, very slowly, worship my cock as if it was your master's."

Marissa obeyed, pulling the fabric down past his penis, which was long and thick, and very smooth. He smelled like citrus and musk with a hint of clove. She wanted to inhale him. But she also wanted to impress him, to make him fall madly in love, if not with her, at least with her talents, which were considerable.

Using her best technique, she forced herself to go slowly, to torture him as he'd tortured her for days now, to inflame him with desire. His cock did respond, swelling and lengthening to her skillful touch. His voice was flat, though, as he said, "Now, kneel up, keep my cock in your mouth and play with your pussy."

Though she was momentarily dismayed by his apparent lack of interest, she scrambled up to do as he ordered, delighted to be able to touch herself at last! Despite constant stimulation, she hadn't been allowed to come since that first day when she'd "stolen" her pleasure. Her fingers found their target and she was, predictably, sopping wet.

This was a place where Marissa was totally comfortable, on her knees with a man's cock down her throat and her fingers buried in her pussy. No one needed to teach her anything here—she had spent years perfecting this particular technique.

Her mouth teased and caressed, withdrew and promised, withheld and gave, while her own fingers brought her close to release, forcing her sighs around the edges of the sizable cock between her lips. She was waiting for his surrender, for the moans, for the cries, for her name to be spoken in a cracked voice of complete and urgent need.

Instead he remained still, hands on his hips, watching her, his expression inscrutable. She forgot to worry, though, as her own pleasure mounted and she rose on the crest of lovely sensation caused by her fingers and his musky scent in her nostrils, his erect cock in her control. Oh, she was going to come. "Stop."

His voice was hard, controlled. Dimly she became aware he was speaking when again he said, "Stop. Take your fingers away, focus only on me." Reluctantly, very reluctantly, she obeyed, almost in tears, so great was her need for release. Of course, part of her had expected it, this was their game here, to keep her always on the edge.

Skillfully, she focused on his cock, teasing it, making love to it as if her life depended on it. Still he didn't move, or sigh or close his eyes. Disconcerted, she tried harder, and must have been a little too rough because he said, "Gently. It isn't a hot dog, it's your master's cock. Worship it, don't bite it off!" Stung, she tried to relax and let her own natural skill take over. What was wrong with this man? Was he gay? She had never encountered another man who could resist her so completely and for so long! Was she losing her touch?

"Play with yourself. Make yourself come." It was an order, cold and precise. Dutifully now, though with less passion, she rubbed her own clit and inserted a finger into her wet and needy pussy. Soon she was back again on that wave of desire, her eyes closed, her moans soft and sweet. He had told her to come, and she would at last! The delicious sensations filled her and she wished desperately it was his cock, instead of her own little finger that filled her pussy.

"Fuck me," she whispered, not even aware she had spoken aloud. Aaron pulled away, watching her.

"Come," he ordered, his voice hard. She did, falling on her side, her fingers swirling in a fever of passion, her eyes shut, her mouth open, lips glistening, gasps of pleasure as she took what she could get. By the time she opened her eyes, he was gone.

What had gone wrong? Who was this girl? This impossible little brat who was getting under his skin and making him almost forget his duties as trainer? God, how close he had come to doing what she asked! To fucking her as she sweetly begged, her voice husky with desire. She was so beautiful, so perfect! It wasn't fair!

It had taken all of Aaron's considerable control not to fall to his knees, to moan, and cry and beg Marissa — to what? To be his love? This was beyond ridiculous. He was used to skilled blowjobs. He was used to withstanding the most delicate touch, the most skilled efforts to draw his essence from him. He truly hadn't expected the flash, the surge of very real desire when those luscious lips closed around his cock. His intention was to bring her to the edge, to keep her focused on service while exhibiting passion, to train her in the art of being a submissive slut. But, my God, she didn't need any lessons!

Why had he chosen himself as her object of desire? Why hadn't he called in Scott? He told himself it was so he could more accurately gauge her reactions, but he knew it was a lie. He had wanted to feel those lips — that tongue — enfold and suckle him as he had watched her do to Scott and to the impervious Frank who was indifferent to her beauty, but still responded to her touch.

He had been so close to coming! And watching her come, watching the blood suffuse her cheeks, the distended nipples, the long, slender fingers buried in her own pussy. He shuddered now as he saw it again in his mind's eye. He was sitting in his study, his penis properly tucked back into his pants, zipper up, hands rigid on his desk.

"This isn't a punishment. I'm going to whip you, because I want to see what you can take. It can be a lovely dance, you know, watching the slave writhe and move under the whip. It's a very intimate thing, between a master and his possession. Tell me, Marissa, does your owner whip you often?" He didn't say master and the omission was a conscious one. From what he'd observed of Tom Reed and of Marissa, Tom was not her master. At least not yet. It was his job to train her to be more receptive to Tom's mastery of her.

And so he continued. "I'm going to use the flogger today. This one has rather short tresses, which I like because it makes for better aim. But it's thick and the leather is soft. It's rather like a caress at first. That's what you like, isn't it?"

Marissa nodded. She couldn't see Aaron because she was blindfolded. Claudette had prepared her for this session. She was standing almost on tiptoe, in the center of the exercise room. Her cuffed wrists were secured to chains that dangled from the ceiling and had been ratcheted up so she was stretched into an X, her legs spread apart and secured by ankle cuffs and clips to thick eyehooks placed strategically in the floor.

Claudette had rouged Marissa's nipples and her mouth, so she looked like a Parisian whore, bound and ready for her whipping, naked and stretched taut. Her pussy was neatly groomed and trimmed, under Claudette's strict dictates. Her breasts were erect and pulled high by her raised arms, a cascade of copper waves tumbling around her face and shoulders. The chains forced her to arch her back and stick out that luscious ass, which seemed to fairly beg for the whip. Her perfect image was reflected endlessly from all angles in the mirrored walls, making Aaron almost dizzy with suppressed desire.

"Have you ever been whipped properly with a flogger, Marissa?"

"Yes, sir. That is, I think so." Tom had whipped her, but the strokes rarely provoked more than a whimper, their tresses more often caressing than biting the flesh.

"We shall see. We shall see," murmured Aaron, reasonably certain she had not. He began the whipping slowly, starting with her ass, increasing the intensity, gauging her reaction by her moans and sighs. She jumped when the lash kissed her back. She wasn't used to that, he could see. Good. Alternating between ass and back, he began to hit her harder, watching the skin redden under the lash. She was breathing rapidly now and jerking with each strike. Her moans had changed to yelps and she was no longer controlling her movements, no longer obviously trying to look sexy. Instead she was jerking away, pulling hard on the chains that bound her.

"Do you want me to stop? Can't take even a little whipping, can you? Only used to the pretend whippings your little boyfriend gave you, eh? Never learned to take it with grace, eh?" He punctuated the last word with a particularly savage blow to her beautiful ass, contempt in his tone. Marissa screamed, but didn't beg him to stop, which surprised him. He'd had her pegged to start begging by now, if not sooner.

Instead a peculiar thing began to happen. As he continued his rhythmic whipping to her ass and back, the jerking and cries slowly faded and Marissa stilled, her breathing slowing. Her head fell back, the hair streaming like liquid bronze down her back and her lips parted, as if she was waiting for a kiss.

Aaron continued to whip her, a steady staccato of leather raining against firm flesh. He was aware what was happening—he had seen it before, though not often. The pain had transmuted to pleasure, an alchemy of feelings at once excruciating and exquisite. Marissa was at the wonderful, dangerous point where she no longer knew pain from pleasure. They truly had become one. She was flying, lost in submissive ether where all judgment was suspended, and one was entirely dependent on the wielder of the whip to know when to stop.

Oh, this wouldn't do. This was where a lover took his slave girl. Not where a trainer took his charge. To snap her out of it and to control his own urge to let her down and fuck her right there on the hardwood floor, he stopped the whipping, and said, his voice harsh, "Marissa!"

She murmured and let her head fall even further back, still lost in the secret, erotic zone. "Marissa!" he barked again, this time removing the blindfold. She blinked in the light and slowly lifted her head, the veil of sexual lethargy falling away. *Good, that was better.* He dropped the whip and picked up a little single-lashed stinger. Whoosh, down on her ass and immediately a long pink line appeared, a fraction of a second later Marissa screamed as the pain zinged to her brain, snapping her completely out of the trance.

He used the little stinger against her ass until he was completely satisfied she was fully recovered from her little "vacation". Until he was completely sure *he* was fully recovered from his own ridiculous transgression, his own absurd desire to possess that which could never be his. He didn't let her down, he didn't want to touch that soft skin, those long, lean limbs. Instead he left her there, sending for a house slave to release her.

Chapter Eight

"Here. Put this on. We get to wear makeup and get all dressed up. It's been a while since we've had a party! I'm so excited!" Amy was grinning widely as she stood next to Marissa in the bathroom. They were sharing the facilities, as were the other slaves, paired in various other bathrooms throughout the spacious mansion. Amy handed Marissa a dark pink corset. Marissa held it up, musing aloud, "I'll never fit in this thing. What is it, a size one?"

"I'll help you. It'll fit, it's supposed to be tight. André likes us girls to get dressed up like French whores. Well, fancy Parisian call girls, more like, I guess. Reminds him of home." Amy grinned. "He chooses the costumes we wear to these parties. Sometimes he invites outsiders and he likes to show us all off. But don't be fooled by the party atmosphere—we're expected to behave with perfect submission and boy do we get it later if we don't!" Amy rubbed her bottom, her eyes squinting as if remembering some particularly brutal punishment.

"You slaves-in-training get your own special assignments. You'll see!" She grinned mischievously.

"What? What do we have to do?"

"Oh, no, I'm not giving it away! That would be telling! Don't worry. It's a blast. It's a party! Now focus on what we're doing. I can never keep track of time and if we don't hurry, we'll be late!"

Amy who was still in her loose, soft shift helped
Marissa put on the little satin corset. Placing her foot
strategically on Marissa's bottom, she pulled at the strings
behind her to tighten the corset as far as it would go. She
laughingly refused any of Marissa's efforts to find out
more details about the upcoming festivities and Marissa
gave up, focusing instead on still being able to breathe as
Amy pulled her corset tighter and tighter. "God, I feel like
Scarlett O'Hara! This is crazy!" Marissa complained, but
when she caught sight of herself in the mirror she stopped.
"Wow," was all she came up with.

Her normally size B breasts looked like Cs or Ds,
pushed up and together, spilling provocatively out of the
little pink satin cups of the corset's bra. Her waist, always
trim, was cinched in, wasp-tight, her hips flaring out to
make even her girlish figure look lush and voluptuous.
"Yeah," Amy laughed. "It may keep you from breathing
but it sure looks hot! Here are stockings, be careful because
they run if you even breathe on them funny. And then you
put this pretty skirt over it so they can take it off later."
She winked.

Marissa took the stockings, carefully rolling the sheer
silk over her calves and thighs then hooking the little
clasps of the garters that dangled from the corset. The skirt
was sheer, little more than a wrap of soft pink silk,
suggestive of the outfits of harem girls or belly dancers. It
was secured only by a long, silky belt attached to the
waist. Little pink satin slippers completed the ensemble.

Amy meanwhile was putting on her own outfit, which
consisted of a black leather bodysuit. The cups of the bra,
however, consisted only of underwire, which held up
Amy's large, lovely breasts, leaving them completely
exposed, the nipples dark and full. There was also a hole

strategically placed at the crotch, to allow access to the slave girl's secret places. She had been allowed to remove her chastity belt for the event. Six-inch stilettos of black leather made the already tall Amy look like a female warrior in some science-fiction sex tale, ready to do battle—or in this case—submit to whatever delicious tortures her masters and their friends came up with.

Marissa helped Amy pull her hair back in a chignon while Amy prattled on about adventures from past parties. To Marissa it almost felt like two girls having a sleepover and playing dress up, until she remembered the import of what they were doing. They were going to be the "toys" at this very adult party and she didn't have any say in the matter.

"We have these parties about once a month. If you're in good standing, that is, you haven't done anything stupid to get yourself punished, you get to go. André and Frank pick out the costumes, and the masters invite some of their select friends and clientele, and *we* are the entertainment! I love it! I get more attention on party night than the whole month! There's this guy, oh, he's so hot, his name is Richard. I hope so bad he'll be there! He's been twice before, but he always has this girl with him. This mousy little slut named Barbara. Still, he always paid a lot of attention to me anyway, and he has like this huge cock, really huge, and I got to suck it last time, I made him beg for it!" She amended, "Well, not actually beg, not out loud, but his eyes said it all, and when he came, he shot his sexy load all over my face and tits, and then made that stupid bitch Barbara lick it off!" Amy laughed happily at the memory. Then she sighed and said, "We better get moving. André likes to inspect us before his guests arrive." They finished applying their makeup, deciding

Marissa should keep her long hair down, and Amy led the nervous girl to the floor below for inspection.

André's office was quite different in temperament from Michael's. Where Michael's was cluttered and warm, André's was spare, the lines long and elegant, very Frank Lloyd Wright. As Amy and Marissa rushed in, André was already inspecting his charges. "You are late, as usual, Amy. And you, Marissa, are you taking after our most irresponsible and naughty slave?" He looked sternly at Marissa who swallowed, not seeing the twinkle in his eye. On party night André was positively giddy, he loved it as much as the slaves did.

Marissa and Amy joined the line of house slaves standing smartly at attention. Frank was first, standing near André's cherry wood desk, which had nothing on its surface but an elegant Art Deco pen and pencil set in a stand. Frank was dressed only in a codpiece of black leather secured over his cock and balls. From his nipples, which were pierced, dangled two gold hoops, attached to each other by a long, thin gold chain that hung now against his strong, well-muscled chest.

Marissa, stealing a glance at him, noticed he seemed to actually shimmer with golden highlights on his skin. She realized he actually *was* golden. He had been painted with gold body paint that made him look like some kind of gorgeous male sprite from some magical forest. Though she didn't like him, she couldn't deny the effect was very striking.

Next to Frank stood little Anne, clad in a long white gown of the finest lace. It was cut tight at the breast and very low, so the tops of her nipples were exposed. Her hair was pulled back, held in place with a white lace band that matched her dress. Her lips were painted a dark red, and her lashes were thick and dark against her fair cheeks as she looked down at the floor, as befitted her station, which she never seemed to forget.

Scott stood next to her, and even he cleaned up rather well, Marissa thought, suppressing a smile. He was dressed in a pirate's silk shirt with ballooning sleeves, opened low on the chest but loose enough to conceal his chubbiness. His pants were black leather, cut close to accentuate his endowment. Around his head a red pirate's scarf was tied rakishly — it matched his red belt.

Tara was next, dressed in a deep red satin gown with plunging neckline. She wore a choker of the same material around her throat and had matching bracelets on either wrist. Little metal loops had been sewn into the choker and bracelets, and use of these would surely be made later.

The other two slave trainees were also there. They were both dressed as Marissa was in tight-fitting corsets and the sheer skirts. Diane's was royal blue and Theresa's an emerald green.

André walked slowly up and down the line as if inspecting a military corps. He straightened a sleeve here, adjusted a collar there and made recommendations for improvement or change. Stopping in front of Marissa, he paused, looking at her critically. "That corset gives you the illusion of voluptuousness," he observed insultingly, adding, "You certainly have a lot of hair, don't you? Quite unusual color, isn't it?" Marissa blushed, annoyed to be singled out and criticized. So her tits weren't huge like Amy's and Diane's. It was the rare man who didn't like them just fine! But of course, she reminded herself, André's gay, so what does he know? And people always loved her hair! What was his problem? She realized suddenly he'd asked a direct question but hoped it was rhetorical, as she had failed to respond.

Apparently no response was expected as he passed on down the line and finally sat at his desk. Looking up at the young men and women before him he said, "Tonight's party will be an excellent opportunity for our slaves-in-training to submit with grace to whatever awaits them. And for the rest of you, I expect the usual degree of complete obedience and servitude." He looked sternly from slave to slave and then laughing, he said, "And don't forget the most important thing of all! Fun! Let's have fun, *mes enfants*! See you at eight."

As he left the room, Amy turned toward Marissa and said, "I told you. The guy is crazy about this party!" Turning to Frank she said, her tone elaborately casual, "So who's coming, Frank? You have the inside scoop, fill us in."

Frank, looking self-important, said, "Oh, the usual perverts and big wheeler-dealers. There's a guy from France coming in, an old friend of André's who wants to meet *me*. And let's see, Mary Ann and her little slave girl will be there. And Mark Reinharz, the whip maker! He wants to carry some of our stuff in his catalog!" Amy tapped her foot, looking nervous and impatient, but saying nothing. Finally he relented and said, "Oh, yes, and one other guest—Richard Forsyth."

Amy's face flooded with happiness and relief, but then she frowned and said, "Just Richard? Or Richard and his appendage, that insufferable little Barbara?"

"Oh, her?" Frank said, fully aware of the effect his words would have on Amy. "She's yesterday's news, Amy. Richard is footloose and fancy-free. And who knows, maybe he's in the market for big dyke sluts who can't keep their panties on!" Laughing derisively, he swept out of the room, looking regal in spite of the fact he was practically naked.

The spacious front room was elegantly appointed with large comfortable couches and high-backed Queen Anne chairs, their cushions lushly upholstered in striped silk. The color scheme was warm gold and crimson. Seated about the room were the masters and their guests. In addition to André, Michael and Claudette, the French guest Louis, Mark the whip maker, a dominatrix named Mary Ann and Amy's heartthrob Richard were seated on various couches and chairs.

Claudette was dressed in a gown of silver that exactly matched her hair and the effect was simple but stunning. She sat on an overstuffed couch with Anne kneeling next to her, massaging her feet. Claudette's hand rested lightly on Anne's head and the affection between them was clear.

At Mistress Mary Ann's feet was a young woman named Beth who was dressed in crisscrossing strips of black leather that completely exposed and accentuated her breasts and shaved pussy. She wore a heavy dog collar, to which a leash was attached, held loosely in her mistress' lap. Her mistress was a regal-looking woman with fiery red hair, wearing a tight-fitting red leather pantsuit with a halter-top.

The main attraction was in the center of the room, though no one at the moment seemed to be paying the slightest bit of attention. The three slave trainees were standing at attention on a raised dais. They stood stiffly, eyes on the horizon, as the position prescribed, each stuffed into her little corset, harem silks flowing. Their faces were various shades of red, all three embarrassed and shy to be displayed thus.

Louis and Mark were engaged in conversation with André. Frank stood nearby, holding a tray of champagne, his body glimmering gold in the soft light. Tara and Scott were offering food and drink to the guests. Amy came around with a tray of stuffed mushrooms. She stopped shyly in front of Richard who took one and then another, stuffing them in his mouth and announcing, "These are outstanding! My compliments to the chef!" Amy, being the chef, blushed prettily and smiled at him. Richard was a big man, tall and large, his girth ample but not flabby. When he stood, he towered over Amy, which not many men did.

Now Richard gestured to Amy to come closer and when she did, he told her to put the tray down on the little table next to his chair. Pulling her toward him, she landed on his lap. With a big belly laugh, he leaned forward, rubbing his large head between her uplifted bare breasts, making a sound of joy. She giggled and grabbed his head, hugging him against her. Pointing toward the dais, Richard lifted his head and leaned toward her ear, whispering.

At that moment André approached the dais and cleared his throat. "Ladies and gentlemen. May I have your attention? As you can see, we have three lovely slave girls displayed for your amusement tonight. Each one will curtsey as I introduce her," he said, looking meaningfully at the three girls to indicate that they should obey.

"First, Theresa. She is as submissive as she is lovely and very willing and eager to serve you. She has been highly trained in the sadistic arts and can take quite a whipping." Theresa curtsied gracefully, her head bowed. "Next, Diane who is a good little slave, but was rather shy, shall we say, when she was placed in our care. She has been learning about the pleasures of erotic submission.

Tonight would be an excellent opportunity for anyone so inclined to try out her new skills in the sexual arena." He smiled as Diane curtsied, blushing hotly.

"And finally, our newest addition, Marissa. She's not especially submissive but she has been making some progress. Perhaps tonight one of you can help her to appreciate the value of obeying without question. Or perhaps you can just use her and throw her back—we'll clean her up, don't worry." He laughed, and several of the guests tittered along with him. Marissa curtsied, furious that she had been described so insultingly. "Take your time, enjoy the food our slaves have prepared and in a little while the auction will begin."

The auction! Why hadn't anyone told her about this auction thing? She felt like some kind of mannequin on display on the raised little stage as people casually looked her over. Obviously the slaves-in-training were tonight's attraction, and she was expected to provide the entertainment to this motley crew of perverts and sadists. And yet, if she was totally honest, a part of her thrilled to be up on display, dressed in these sexy and very flattering garments. She knew she looked fantastic, far better than the overweight Diane and the scrawny little Theresa. Daring to move her focus from the far wall, she stole a gaze around the room.

Where was he? Was he too high and mighty to come to their little play-parties? She saw Michael and Claudette sitting together on a couch, she leaning into him, he with his arm around her. Little Anne knelt next to them, sipping a long, thin flute of champagne that made Marissa's mouth purse. She could almost taste the dry bubbly tart-sweetness.

Slowly her eyes scanned the large room. Everyone else from the house was there, except Aaron. How long was she supposed to stand up here anyway? That champagne looked wonderful, and Scott and Tara were still walking around the room with little silver trays loaded with delicious-looking little savories. Marissa's mouth started to water.

She was distracted, though, by the door opening. Aaron entered at last and Marissa couldn't suppress the happy little smile that bloomed on her lips. Tonight he wasn't wearing his usual uniform of jeans and button-down linen shirt. Instead he was wearing caramel-colored brown leather pants that seemed molded to his long, strong thighs. A matching leather vest covered a heavy T-shirt, the sleeves cut short against bulging biceps. Marissa noticed with sudden irritation that all the women and several of the men were eyeing him with the same lustful desire she was.

Aaron seemed unaware of the stir he was causing as he walked directly up to the dais, shaking his head when Tara offered him a little sweet and sour shrimp. André excused himself from his animated conversation with the whip maker to again approach the dais. "Ahem. Excuse me. If you are ready, our auctioneer has arrived." André smiled toward Aaron who nodded at him. "Aaron, as you all know, has been working intensively with each one of these lovely women and he is now eager to share the fruits of his labor with you. Aaron, if you will?"

Aaron moved to the front of the dais. Leaning toward the girls he said quietly, "Good evening, ladies. As you have no doubt become aware, you are this evening's entertainment. I expect each of you to behave with the submission and grace I know you possess. I'm going to offer you for the bidding—it's just in fun, of course. They are only 'buying' the pleasure of your submission for the evening, but I expect you to behave as if this was the real thing. Whatever is asked of you, you do it. Obey without hesitation. Everyone here is a professional and you won't be endangered. In fact, you might even have fun!" He winked at Diane who looked away, fidgeting. She was certainly the most uncomfortable in the tight corset, which cut into the roll of flesh under her arms. It was strung so tightly her ample figure was compressed into a pleasing hourglass shape, but she was sweating, the sheen of perspiration glowing lightly on her face.

Turning back to his audience, Aaron said in a louder voice, "The bidding is begun. Is there an offer?" While Aaron had been talking to the girls, Frank had handed out paper play-money to all the guests. They held the brightly colored bills, attention eagerly focused on the three slave girls.

Richard sat up, Amy now kneeling next to his chair. "One hundred for Diane!" he shouted, his voice booming.

"Two hundred," Mary Ann, the dominatrix, countered.

"Three hundred," Richard called, and Diane blushed, looking nervous but happy this attention was being paid to her. The bidding went on and when Richard reached one thousand, Mary Ann graciously bowed toward him in a gesture of polite defeat, Diane was helped down from the dais and given over to the welcoming arms of Richard and Amy.

Aaron gestured toward the two remaining slave girls and Mark the whip maker piped up, "Let's cut right to it. I want that girl to test my new single lash out. One thousand for Theresa!" There was no contest, as no one had been given more than a thousand in play-money, and so Theresa was led to the little group that comprised Mark, André and Frank.

Marissa stood alone now on the dais. Could the "auctioneer" bid on the girls? Well, if he could, he didn't. There was a lively contest between Louis and Mary Ann, but Louis acquiesced graciously to Mary Ann in the end, since he was in fact rather keen on watching Theresa's whipping.

A slightly stunned Marissa was escorted off the dais by Aaron who led her to Mary Ann, still sitting regally in her chair, her little slave girl collared and leashed at her feet. Marissa looked up at Aaron, a pleading expression on her face but he only looked back at her impassively. Then he whispered, "Don't shame me, slave. Do whatever you're told. Consider it a lesson." Bowing her head, Marissa knelt in front of Mary Ann, her eyes on Mary Ann's stiletto heels, her fingers twisting nervously together behind her back.

His official duties completed, Aaron sat down on a chair, observing the room. The group of men with Theresa already had her stripped and bent in a punishment position. Louis was feeling her flanks and André was lecturing about the proper use of the single lash. Her face was obscured but Aaron knew she was in her element. She had not only gotten over her fear of the cane and single lash, she had come to crave the stinging kiss, and Aaron knew his job with her was complete. She would go home to serve her master/husband, and he could now use her without fear.

Diane was not serving anyone at the moment, but was instead herself the center of attention with the man who had purchased her for the evening. Amy was directing

Diane to sit on the chair Richard had been sitting in a moment before. After untying the silky little skirt and tossing it aside, Amy directed Diane to spread her ample thighs, displaying her bare and shaven pussy to the gentleman who now knelt before her. Diane blushed a hot beet red as he leaned forward and began to tongue her pussy, while Amy held her arms from behind the chair. Diane's month of training was nearing its end and she was not only no longer shy about sex, she had discovered the delicious pleasures of oral sex and of a budding bisexuality under Aaron's and Amy's careful tutelage. But she wasn't used to a man's tongue between her legs, in the past she had always refused her master's attempts, begging him to understand a slave girl didn't deserve that kind of attention.

Aaron had taught her a slave girl deserved whatever attentions those whom she served deemed appropriate. It wasn't up to her. And Amy had finally truly convinced her through words and action that she wasn't "stinky down there" and that men—and women—really did find her sexy and desirable. With just a little more practice and time to get used to her newfound confidence as a sex kitten, Aaron could consider her a success as well.

Ah, there was Marissa, kneeling now in front of Mary Ann and her little slave girl. Any chance of success? Perhaps it was too early to call. She was less than a week into her training. But he had been met with resistance at every turn. His first premonition that she was not submissive, but merely masochistic and highly sexed, seemed to be winning out. She clearly had an agenda and wanted to seem to be succeeding, to appear to be submitting.

He was fairly certain it was simply a matter of economics in the end. She wanted someone to take care of her and that person wanted her to behave submissively. Who was he to decide if this was morally bereft or simply "the real world"? Aaron accepted the glass of fine French champagne Scott offered him. "Bring me the bottle," he said.

Aaron sat alone, drinking his cold champagne, taking in the little vignettes of orgiastic play and torture. Louis had wandered from the whipping and was now watching Tara and Scott remove their clothing for his amusement. He would probably take them into one of the guest suites soon—Louis liked to watch but he didn't like others watching him.

Claudette and Michael were leaning toward one another, talking softly. They'd been together for years and her complete submission to him was unquestioned and supremely romantic. Aaron yearned for a connection like that, but realized it probably wasn't in the cards. He was too guarded to ever get that close to someone again. Taking a deep drink from the flute, Aaron watched Diane being adored by Richard and Amy, both of whom were almost naked now themselves and completely at ease in their hedonistic joy. Aaron admired that sort of freedom in theory, but for himself found it immodest.

Finally, as if only allowing his eyes the thing they really sought after they'd "done their duty" by watching the other players, Aaron let his gaze settle again on the threesome that included Marissa. What he saw didn't surprise him, but the little jolt of jealous heat that rushed through his veins did. Marissa was sitting on Mary Ann's lap, her arms pinned behind her by the dominatrix, while the little slave girl at their feet knelt between Marissa's legs, licking and suckling her spread pussy. The mistress was letting a lash fall against her slave's back with casual flicks, urging her on in her task with the whip.

Marissa was flushed and Aaron could see the little slave girl knew just what she was doing. His own image crouching there between Marissa's legs flashed before his consciousness for a second but it was so fast even he didn't see it. Instead he watched as Mary Ann pulled Marissa's head back so their mouths were touching. He saw her kiss Marissa's lips, forcing her tongue into the girl's mouth. He saw Marissa's initial resistance and then surrender.

Mary Ann let her go, again whipping her little slave girl as the girl bent over Marissa's sex. Marissa's eyes were closed and her head fell back against Mary Ann who held her tight on her lap. Aaron was staring straight at Marissa when suddenly she opened her eyes and focused straight on him. Their eyes locked for a moment. There was almost a physical connection between them, something electric, something dangerous. Aaron was the first one to turn his gaze away.

Shortly afterwards he left the party, slipping out unseen, except, of course, by Marissa.

Maybe it was time to get out. When the slaves-in-training could get to you like this, you were losing your edge. It was becoming personal, and that, Aaron knew, was the end for any successful trainer. These women were on loan, if you will. She belonged to another, and he had entrusted Aaron to mold her, to shape her into a submissive slave and then return her, intact and ready to serve. Instead Aaron found himself the one becoming enslaved!

He had to focus. He had to remove the allure, the desire. He would focus on the punishment aspects. He would leave any sexual training to others. He would work with Marissa in the area where she truly needed shaping, which was submission and duty. She still basically only did what she wanted when she wanted. Every act that embarrassed or humiliated her was met with resistance and a fight. He would bring her down. He would knock that arrogance out of her and hand her back, with relief, to her owner.

Then he'd take a long vacation and figure out where his head was at. Go back to England and see his family. Get far away from Le Chateau L'Esclave and the beautiful, strange woman who had entered his life.

A plan was forming in his mind, he'd meet with Marissa's owner, with Tom Reed, and get his permission to properly humble the girl. With a resolute expression, Aaron went to see Michael and make his proposal.

Chapter Nine

Tom crossed his legs, leaning back in his chair. Aaron and André sat across from him at The Club. Six days had passed, and he hadn't seen or spoken to Marissa, though he'd thought of little else during his spare moments. Twelve-hour workdays had provided enough distraction as he busied himself with other people's money and how to make more of it, to at least allow him to resist the impulse to drive up to Westchester and collect Marissa at once.

He had spoken with Michael every day, and been assured progress was being made, and that Marissa was settling in nicely, though some adjustment was necessary. But today, it was Michael who had called him. He had explained they were meeting with a "certain resistance" from Marissa. "She is not, I am afraid, submissive, strictly speaking. That is something I think you knew going in, Mr. Reed, am I correct?" Tom had to admit it was, but hope springs eternal.

"Are you saying it's hopeless? She isn't 'trainable'?" Tom felt annoyed, embarrassed and angry that Marissa wasn't performing up to snuff. Secretly though, had he been honest, he wasn't surprised.

"Not at all. No one is hopeless. But her trainer Aaron thinks perhaps more, uh, drastic measures are in order. If we are to continue, that is. I think you and Aaron should meet. He can fill you in completely.

"And it's time for your training as well. You know we spoke about certain basic technique, the use of a cane, that sort of thing. We want to familiarize you with what Marissa has been learning, with the names of positions and how she is being taught to respond to your commands. With your permission, I'll have Aaron call you right away and you can schedule a meeting and decide at that time how to proceed with your hands-on training as well."

Tom wasn't sure how he felt about this "hands-on" stuff. He knew what he needed to dominate a woman, didn't he? It was by instinct, to his way of thinking. On the other hand, he had never used a cane and was very interested in learning to do so. He certainly didn't want to permanently mark his slave girl or do anything dangerous. They could show him that much, anyway. And he'd listen to whatever else they had to say. He'd found in business sometimes one learned the most when not looking for it, just by keeping mouth shut and ears open.

True to Michael's word, Aaron called later that afternoon and an appointment was made for the next day. Aaron suggested he and André come down to the city and Tom agreed, though he had been hoping to go up to the castle to catch a glimpse of Marissa. But probably it was better this way. Now the trainer sat across from him, the man who had been "teaching" his girlfriend to submit and doing God knew what to her to get her to obey. Even though Tom had hired these guys and paid good money for them to use and abuse his slave girl, his feelings were definitely ambivalent at this point.

André, used to dealing with clients much more than Aaron, took the lead. "First, Tom, let's address your issues. This is your time. We want to answer any and all questions you have. And Aaron would like to make some suggestions as well. This is an open forum so we can provide the best possible training for your slave. And afterwards, our own little Anne is down in the dungeon, and we could go over some techniques with the cane and other things, if you have the time. You may remember Anne, one of our house slaves."

Tom sat up, and blurted, "Anne?" Her image popped into his head. The honey blonde hair, the downcast eyes, big and blue, the small perfect breasts with the little gold hoops that had been so sweetly exposed to him at Claudette's insistence. He felt a tightening in his balls and shifted again in his seat, forcing his face into a neutral expression. His voice did not betray his excitement as he said, "I see. Yes, well, that would be good, I guess. I do want to learn to use the cane properly."

"Excellent," André murmured, and they turned to the discussion of Marissa's training. Aaron explained in some detail about the different aspects of the regime they had previously agreed to and how it was going for Marissa. He gave examples of where she was progressing and where things had stalled.

"I'll be perfectly blunt, Mr. Reed." Aaron said, spreading his long fingers flat on the table between them. "She's too proud. She's gorgeous and she knows it, and is used to using that beauty to her advantage. I've tried to humble her, to bring her down to the level suitable for a slave, but it hasn't been easy. And with barely a week left, I'd like to make a suggestion. It's rather radical but it's not permanent, and I really think the psychological effect might be what's needed here."

"What?" Tom was curious. He knew Marissa was proud and that she had traded on her good looks and confidence all her life to get her what she wanted. Unbidden, he thought of Anne again, waiting demurely downstairs, perhaps naked? Perhaps chained to one of the many instruments of torture and bondage they had down in the well-equipped play chambers? She was beautiful, too, in her own quiet way. Where Marissa captured the attention in the room, stopping conversations with her striking beauty and model's confidence, Anne would slip in, easing stealthily into the heart, her sensitive dreamer's face glowing with some kind of inner serenity. Guiltily Tom forced his attention back to what Aaron was saying. What was wrong with him?

"I have a few ideas. How to humble the girl, make her more open to training. I think we ought to shave her head. All her hair, in fact. Denude her. That hair is an emblem. A symbol of her feminine beauty. Her trademark. Shave it off, like a prisoner. Leave her truly naked. And instead of leaving her physically nude as we usually do during the course of training, we will clothe her. In a modern-day sackcloth, if you will. In an unflattering housedress of polyester. Instead of allowing her to flaunt her perfect body and model's hair, let's strip her of that physical pride at least. The psychological effect could be dramatic. I think it will be. What do you think?"

Tom was taken aback by the suggestion at first. His Marissa, with a bald head and bare pussy? It would be like shaving a Persian cat. She would look, well, ridiculous. But he supposed that was the idea. Wouldn't she balk at that, though? "She'd never agree," he said out loud.

"It isn't up to her. She's signed the contract. With your permission, of course, we would force her. I think she would comply with the proper, uh, inducements. I also think she should be moved out of her bedroom and down to the slave quarters in the dungeons. She should sleep on a cot and be constantly reminded of her position. Right now she's like a spoiled little princess up there, which is a role she knows all too well."

Aaron leaned forward to Tom, his face earnest. "Listen, let me be completely frank. If you want a girl who simply plays at submission, do nothing. If you want a trained slave, along the lines of Anne who is waiting downstairs for you to whip her, then take my advice."

Slowly Tom nodded. He tried to focus on what Aaron was saying, knowing it was important to pay attention and make a decision. But truth to tell, at the mention of Anne, the image of Marissa had faded from his mind, replaced with the lovely little girl downstairs. He would learn to use the cane—for Marissa—of course. He wasn't doing this because he wanted Anne, it was for Marissa. He stood, nodding again. "Do it. Shave her head. Do whatever you have to do. Now let's go down and see about this caning." He was almost loping toward the dungeon door, his expression eager, Marissa forgotten. André and Aaron exchanged looks, André's knowing and cynical, Aaron's bemused.

Anne was waiting for her masters. She was the only person in the dungeon, since it was midafternoon on a weekday, not a popular time to use the space. She was kneeling, forehead touching the ground, her face to the far wall, her little bottom lifted prettily up and hands resting loosely at her sides.

She was perfectly still, though she must have heard them come in. "Get up, Anne," André ordered, and Anne rose in one fluid, elegant movement, her small body unfolding in front of them, her back still to them. "Turn around."

As she did so Tom noticed she was gagged and blindfolded. The light caught the little hoops of gold glinting at each nipple. He wanted to tug on them, to pull her by them, to gently bite the soft nubs pierced with gold. She looked so helpless — naked — with her mouth and eyes covered in black silk. His breath caught in his throat. Aaron walked forward and took her hand and Anne followed him, walking with grace and balance even though she could not see where she was going. The trust was implicit and absolute.

As Aaron led her to a padded whipping bar, André opened a long case, which appeared to be a musical instrument case, but in fact, contained many fine whips, crops and canes, most of them designed by himself and fashioned by his slave Frank with great attention to detail, proper weighting and the finest leathers and woods available. He removed a slender cane with a curved, decorated handle. It resembled nothing so much as a very thin umbrella handle.

André, quite proud of his substantial collection of canes, began a little lecture about the cane while Aaron silently directed Anne to bend over and allow herself to be tethered to the whipping bar for the lesson. Tom's eyes were riveted to the small, naked woman, as André explained, "This cane is made of Malaysian rattan. I've found this rattan to be the best material for a cane, because of its flexibility and straightness. We hand sand it and treat it with pure linseed oil. And of course, it's tested, thoroughly, on the flesh of our slaves. Here, you take it."

He handed the cane to Tom, holding it out so Tom could take the handle, which was adorned with a piece of red glass, shaped like a teardrop, secured with thin strips of sterling silver.

"We'll use this shorter cane today, it's easier to handle. You need to always remember to wield it lightly, unlike a heavy flogger you might be used to. See how light it is, how supple. Rattan is better for a milder caning, which we'll be doing here. Bamboo is more effective for actual punishment, when you really want to bring the lesson home, as it were."

As Tom held the cane uncertainly André urged, "Touch it, feel the length, get used to the heft. The weight of a cane is important and here appearances may be deceptive. Rattan is a very light material and inexperienced owners are liable to choose their canes on the slender side, reasoning this will make the strokes more merciful. In fact the reverse is true—a slim, wand-like cane is crueler and more liable to cut. Thicker canes like the one you are holding are less liable to break the skin."

André was warming to his topic, clearly one dear to his heart. As he spoke, naked little Anne remained perfectly still, of course hearing all about the instrument that was about to be used upon her submissively upturned bottom. Her stillness was more than a mere lack of movement. It was an inner control, a peace of the spirit.

"Aaron," André said, "remove her gag. I want to hear her scream."

As Aaron untied the silk covering her mouth, André took the cane back from Tom, ready to demonstrate. "The cane, unlike a whip or paddle, is an instrument of great potential severity and care must be taken when administering it or you will cut the skin. It is also lighter than it looks. But the important point is its extreme flexibility. During the quarter second or so of flight, the instrument achieves a near semi-circularity in shape.

Although it may appear straight and even stiff, in practice it is more whip-like."

Demonstrating in the air, André continued. "The arm and wrist motion is therefore a complex one. At the beginning of the stroke, the hand leads the tip of the cane, it continues to lead throughout the descent, only at the last moment, after the shortest of follow-throughs, does the wrist halt and reverse direction slightly so that the business end of the cane catches at exactly the right angle." As he spoke, André flicked the cane, its whistle echoing in the chamber. Tom flinched at the sound, but Anne didn't move a muscle. "You see," André went on implacably, "the achievement of a good caning action is therefore a matter of some diligence and constant practice."

André continued to lecture, as if discussing how to thread a needle or to build a birdhouse. He seemed completely indifferent to the naked slave bound and bent at his mercy. "Another precaution is to take one's stance slightly to the left of the target—perhaps as much as a half-pace. This ensures the tip of the cane, which travels faster than the rest of the instrument during the latter part of the flight, strikes the far buttock at precisely the same instant and with the same force, as the rest of the cane makes contact with the near buttock. The result should be a perfect stripe across the broadest part of the bottom.

"Like so," he said, and let the cane slice through the air, landing in a long horizontal line across Anne's little rounded bottom. Anne jerked and emitted a little yelp. Tom watched in fascination as a long line of white appeared on her flesh, faded and reappeared as a thin welt of fiery red.

"Now you try, Mr. Reed." André handed the cane to Tom who was trying to remember André's copious advice while staring at the pretty little slave girl bound before him. Aaron stood back impassively, taking in the scene, his strong arms folded across his chest.

Trying not to betray his nervousness, Tom took the offered cane and moved closer to Anne. He wished the two men were not there, observing and critiquing him. "Yes, that's it." André encouraged. "Take a horizontal or even slightly upward aim, draw the cane back slowly, yes, that's it. Now whip the forearm and wrist smartly through from one side to the other, keeping your eyes on the exact spot you are aiming for."

Keeping his eye on the "target", that lovely little ass, Tom tried to follow the instructions and let his cane land smartly on Anne's tender flesh. She screamed and another line, just below the one André had created, appeared in white, faded and bloomed an angry red. Tom looked to André, uncertain, afraid he had overdone it.

But André just nodded, smiling and said, "Continue. Give her another ten strokes." Tom did so, forgetting the men, focusing only on the bound woman who cried out with each lash of his cane. Each little mew and cry served only to harden his already erect cock. She looked so vulnerable and perfect tied down before him, a willing subject to his torture. Her ass was crisscrossed with long, red welts by the time he was done, and Tom found himself elated and curiously exhausted.

Anne was breathing hard and moaning, though it sounded more like sexual arousal to Tom than from pain. He stared at the pattern of welts he had tattooed against her ass and thighs. The sight was wildly erotic. He felt a searing desire to pull her down and fuck her. Fervently he wished neither of the other men were in the room and he could untie her, take her down and ravage her right there on the dungeon floor. The aphrodisiac of having used the cane, of having whipped and marked a naked, willing little slave girl was a powerful one, and it took all his willpower to maintain his self-possessed demeanor. He stood there, his face a mask of control as Aaron let the girl down and caught her as she fell against him. Aaron lifted her gently into his arms.

"That was excellent," André said, smiling at Tom with approval. "You have a natural talent with the cane. You just need to learn confidence, to get used to the heft of it and the damage it can inflict. If anything, you needn't be so tentative. The idea is, after all, to hurt her. So you needn't worry about that. Anne here is a pain slut, aren't you, dear? She loves to be caned. Don't you, Anne?"

"Yes, sir," Anne whispered, as Aaron lowered her carefully to the floor.

"Thank the gentleman for your caning, slave," Aaron ordered her.

"Thank you, sir," Anne whispered. Tom noticed her face was flushed and tears were streaked across the pretty pink cheeks. He'd made her cry! He'd been too rough!

André saw his concern, read it correctly and said, "Put your finger in her cunt, Mr. Reed. Feel how wet she is. As I said, she's a pain slut. She can cry all the pretty tears she wants but she lives for this. It's why she was born, isn't it, cunt?"

Anne, now kneeling down, sore and tender bottom perched on her heels, hands on her thighs, palms up, nodded, though her face was flushed and eyes downcast. Her pussy was accessible and Tom was so aroused by the whole scene that he did as André offered, kneeling down in front of her and tentatively touching her bared and offered sex.

It was sopping. His fingers lingered several seconds longer than necessary, as his cock pushed itself even more erect, bending painfully as it strained against his clothing, longing to be freed to nestle into the sweet, little wet opening. It might have only been his imagination, but he thought she arched ever so slightly against his hand as if she wanted his touch as much as he did. Her eyes were on the floor and he couldn't make out her expression.

He felt her heat and his own desire, and admitted again to himself that he wanted to fuck Anne. This wasn't about caning or about learning a new skill so he could better dominate Marissa. This was about this perfect, charming little submissive creature, dutifully allowing herself to be finger-fucked by a man who had just had a caning technique lesson on her ass. God, he wanted her! And what about Marissa who was supposedly the one he yearned for? Life was getting too fucking complicated!

Pulling his hand away, suddenly aware of the two men observing him with his hand on their slave's pussy, he stood up abruptly. "This was, uh, really interesting," he said stiffly, again wishing them gone, now wishing himself gone, back safe in his own office or bedroom, away from these strange men and their naked charge.

"Indeed," André agreed. "If you have the time tomorrow, Aaron must return to the chateau, but I will be in the city for another day. I can keep Anne, and we can go over the positions Aaron is teaching Marissa. If you are familiar as well, you will only have to use their proper names and Marissa will obey you. Would that suit you, sir?"

Anne would be with him! Oh, yes, that would suit him fine indeed. Forget the meeting with his second largest client. This was more important. He'd see her again tomorrow! Feeling confused, pushing down the feelings of guilt, still telling himself it was for Marissa, Tom agreed to the meeting and left the dungeon, leaving the naked girl still kneeling down, waiting for the bidding of her masters, patience like a mask of peace on her pretty little tear-streaked face.

As Aaron drove home alone, he mused about the afternoon's events. Either he had lost his ability to read a man, or Mr. Reed was falling in love with Anne! Aaron himself barely noticed Anne, except when he needed her to serve him in some capacity. She was part of the furniture — an object. He knew Michael liked to fuck her and to have her play with Claudette for his amusement, but she just wasn't his type. He didn't care for the petite and highly submissive little Anne, though he found no fault with her as a well-trained slave.

No, he liked his women more robust, with more fire, more passion. He liked to break them, like wild fillies, and then keep them reined in. He liked a woman more like — Marissa. Now wasn't this a silly little complication of Shakespearian proportions? He smiled ruefully at himself, admitting at last he was falling in love. Ridiculous! Unheard of!

Well, that wasn't true entirely. He had fallen for a girl, fallen hard, years ago when he first became involved in this rather bizarre business. She belonged to a very wealthy Italian man and she had been as wild and brazen as Marissa, if not more so. He hadn't learned about his own limits yet, and had yielded to the temptation to fuck her, to use her sexually for his own pleasure rather than for her training. She didn't reciprocate his romantic feelings. Instead, she had controlled him through his desire and the training had not been successful. He had finally handed her over to Michael, feeling he had failed. He'd learned then not to give into his own physical desires and, in fact, since then it was rarely an issue.

Aaron was not a man easily won over. It was precisely this exacting and difficult nature which helped make him such a success as a trainer. While not unaware of a woman's wiles, he was mostly indifferent to them. Tall, handsome, rich and smart, he could have his pick of women and did so, when off the job. Why bother to get involved with someone else's toy?

And yet…and yet Marissa was waiting back at the chateau. He had called ahead and ordered she be bound in the dungeon, shackled against the wall for his return. He knew she was waiting and that she was aware he had gone down to the city to see her owner. The owner he had talked into letting Aaron do what was needed with this girl.

Aaron was eager to cut off her pretty hair and dress her in the symbolic "rags" of a frumpy housecoat. That would break some of her impossible pride. He saw the dark, magnificent eyes flashing at him as she refused some simple request, like spreading her ass cheeks. What a silly girl!

Yes, after he shaved her, he would inspect her body, humiliate her all the more. He found himself pushing the gas pedal a little too hard, eager to get home and take care of his Marissa. *Stop*, he admonished himself. *Not yours. A job. That's all she is. In a few days, she'll be gone and that will be the end of that. Focus on the job, not the woman. She belongs to another. And I don't want a slave anyway. Too much work.* He smiled again to himself, shaking his head as he turned up the winding drive to Le Chateau L'Esclave, determined to behave like the professional he knew himself to be.

Aaron entered the dungeon to find Marissa tethered against the wall as instructed. Scott had secured her there, using the middle set of chains and manacles that were embedded in the walls.

When Scott had come to get her, she had been in the middle of a posture lesson with Claudette. As Marissa practiced walking and kneeling with a book on her head, Claudette was lecturing. "A slave should exhibit good posture at all times. You must learn to move gracefully and effortlessly into the positions you've been assigned, whatever they may be. You will need to practice moving from one position to another with this book on your head. Make sure it doesn't fall!" Of course, it did fall, over and over, and each time it did, Marissa received a little swat from Claudette's crop.

Eventually she was getting the hang of it and the crop was used less and less. By the time Scott showed up, Marissa was doing fairly well, though her muscles were aching and she wanted to fling the stupid book at Claudette. At first she was relieved when Scott interrupted, until she heard what he had to say.

"I've just been told to come get Marissa here and take her to the dungeon. She's to be manacled on the dungeon wall. Master Aaron's on his way home." Taking the book from Marissa, Claudette sent them on their way. She looked after the young girl being hurried along by Scott, a curious expression on her face.

Scott refused to talk to her as he led her down to the dungeon. He would only smile knowingly and shake his head when she asked why this was happening and what was going on. Truth to tell, he had no idea what was going on, but he enjoyed acting as if he did and he enjoyed the look of fear and nervousness on Marissa's pretty face.

When they reached the downstairs, he said, "Stand against the wall. Right there. Haven't been down here yet, have you? About time!" Grinning evilly, he pulled her arms up high, securing the cold metal bracelets around her wrists. "Boy, you must have fucked up big time for them to have me do this in the middle of the day. You're gonna get some big ass whipping, I bet. Poor little chickadee." Scott was grinning, hoping he'd get to watch. He was masochistic but also loved to watch others being beaten and tortured. It made his dick hard and he could jerk off so nicely with a fresh image of a beaten slave in his mind's eye.

Maybe he'd even get to fuck this one afterwards, if no one wanted her. The lovely memory of her hot little mouth wrapped around his cock came back to him as his penis engorged and elongated in anticipation. "Too bad we don't have time for a little more oral training, eh, little bitch? Bet you've been dreaming of my cock, haven't you?"

"Fuck you," Marissa hissed, enraged and a little frightened to be at Scott's mercy like this, with no one around to put the reins on him.

Scott's face darkened and he slapped her hard on the cheek. Marissa gasped and turned her face but, of course, she couldn't get away. "You'd be wise to mind your manners, cunt," he snarled, his voice low. "You're not exactly in a position to protest at the moment, are you? No, I'd say you're not in a position to do much of anything right now but take what's coming to you. God, I wish I could fuck you right now. But, unlike *some* people, I'm obedient. I do what I'm told by the masters, and the sooner you learn to, the sooner you'll stop finding yourself in these kinds of situations."

Marissa shut her eyes, willing her mind to go blank, forbidding herself to respond to this little prick who was taunting her. Satisfied he'd made his point, Scott bent down and chained Marissa's ankles to the lower manacles, ratcheting them tightly against her. He stood back and admired the naked woman. She was shivering slightly as it was drafty today in the dungeon. "Cold, darlin'?" Scott asked, his voice falsely intimate as he casually tweaked an erect nipple. "Don't you worry, they'll heat you up good. Maybe I could get you a little warm before they get here. I think I have a little time."

"Leave me alone, please," Marissa begged, truly frightened now, turning her head as he tried to kiss her. Scott pressed up against her, his erection hard against her thigh, his mouth just level with hers.

"And miss this chance to bring you down a notch, you prissy little cunt? No way!" Roughly he forced her lips open with his tongue, holding her head still with his hands on either side of her face, gripping her hair. She twisted and struggled, ignoring the cut of the irons at her wrists and ankles. "Oooh, a vixen!" Scott laughed. "Not much you can do about it now, is there?"

Reaching down, he grabbed her pussy, pulling the pubic hair until she yelped. "Get away from me!" she cried.

"Make me!" he grinned. "You weren't so high and mighty when you had your tongue up my ass, were you?" He laughed cruelly. God, she was hot. Bending over he bit her nipple, twisting it between his teeth as he unzipped his own pants. She cried out. He couldn't fuck her from this angle, and didn't dare let her down but instead rubbed himself against her thigh, like a rutting dog. The nipple popped out of his mouth, red and shiny with his spit as he moved to the other breast, treating it just as savagely.

He rubbed hard and fast, determined to take his pleasure, with no idea how much time he had left. He came within a matter of minutes, groaning loudly as he spurted against Marissa's leg, his face mashed between her breasts. Marissa's face was turned against the wall, her body pressed back as if she could get away from him, just a little. They both heard the sound of boots against the stone stairwell and Scott leaped back, rubbing the semen from her thigh with his shirttail, as he pulled his pants up, moving as quickly as he could.

He just succeeded in zipping his pants under his fat little belly when Aaron rounded the corner and took in the scene, not completely sure what had happened but certain something had. Still, the house rules were clear, and if Scott had taken his pleasure with Marissa, it was his right when he could get it. Irrationally the thought of Scott using Marissa angered Aaron and he snapped at the slave boy, "Get out, you little piece of shit. I'll deal with you later!"

Scott hurried away, leaving Marissa with her head still turned, eyes closed, nipples still glistening and erect in the damp cool air. "What did he do?" She didn't answer and he barked, "Direct question! Answer!"

Slowly Marissa opened her eyes and turned to face him. "He jerked off on my leg like some pathetic little dog. It was beyond disgusting." Her voice dripped with contempt and rage. Aaron smiled grimly. It was disgusting, but it certainly wasn't her place to voice it, and so bluntly.

"Did you thank him?"

"Excuse me?"

"Did you thank him? You are supposed to thank anyone who uses you, whore. You exist to be used, surely you know that. You knew the rules. If you failed to thank Scott, then you've screwed up yet again, little missy." He smiled at her, daring her to protest. He watched the emotions flit over her face, the anger, the disbelief and the actual effort to behave submissively, to control her own impulses. It was as good a time as any to let her know what was coming.

"I went to see your owner today. We had a very long talk. He's agreed you are hopeless at this point and some drastic measures are in order." He paused, staring at her, his expression hard. "He agreed I should cut off your hair and shave your cunt as a symbolic gesture on your part of giving up that pride of yours."

"What!"

"Did I give you permission to speak?"

"You can't be serious! Tom would never want you to do that! He loves my hair!"

"After I do it, I'm going to leave you here and punish you severely, first for speaking repeatedly without being asked to, and second for daring to imply I'm acting without your owner's express permission! Not only am I going to shave your head and pussy, but you are going to wear this lovely garment for the duration of your stay here." He pulled out a dime-store special, a tacky housecoat of orange and green polyester with large metal snaps down the front. Size — large.

Marissa's face was a study in horror as she eyed it. So much of her self-concept and self-worth were bound up in her physical appearance. He had found her Achilles' heel at last. Placing the dress on a cot, he brought out the barber's scissors and little electric trimmer he had procured for the shearing.

"Don't move, girl," he hissed into her ear. "You don't want to get cut. These scissors are very sharp. Stay still." Taking a handful of her hair, he snipped it up high, near her skull, letting a foot of lovely coppery strands fall to the ground. Marissa cried out, begging him to stop, again speaking out of turn, struggling helplessly in her chains.

"Stop! Stop, you bastard! Let me down! Stop, oh, please!" Marissa protested and wrestled against Aaron as best she could while in chains. She cried and begged, but for some reason she never said the words that would have freed her from this torment. She never said, "I want out". She could have and he would have immediately let her down. But she didn't, though Aaron was waiting, listening carefully to the words between the cries. If she said she wanted out of the contract that would be it, it would be over. He found himself holding his breath and mentally chided himself for that. Whatever happened would be fine with him.

Carefully, so as not to hurt the still struggling girl, Aaron cut her hair into a ragged pixie, as close to her head as possible. She looked so young without that wild tousle of sexy hair around her head. Ignoring her tears and threats, he turned on the little whirring shaver and proceeded to shave her shapely head until it was soft and bare as a newborn's.

Her sobs had quieted and she gasped as he reached down and grabbed a little handful of pubic curls, cutting them neatly with the scissors. "Stay very still, Marissa. I don't want to cut your little pussy. Don't move. It'll be over in a minute." Once he'd cut off what he could, he squirted baby oil over the soft, nearly denuded sex and took a fresh tripled-edged razor from his pocket. Flicking away the protective plastic covering, he drew the blades slowly down her mons.

He could feel her heart tapping and thumping against his shoulder as he leaned into her for support. To her credit, she was staying very still, no doubt the fear of getting cut overcame her desire to fend him off. When he was finished, he stood back to see if he'd missed anything and then to admire his handiwork.

She looked impossibly young and vulnerable without the pubic curls and the mane of hair. His instinct was to take her into his arms and kiss away the tears. Instead he wiped her cheeks and nose with a handkerchief he drew from his pocket, and said, "It's done, Marissa. I've cut away your pride. Now you can truly begin to submit, if you're willing."

Chapter Ten

"Oh, my God," Tara said softly. "What did they do to you?" Marissa was actually lightly dozing, her bare head lolling against her shoulder, arms and legs still forcibly extended in an X. She looked so different without the hair! Instead of the gorgeous model, she looked like a child or a spirit. There was something almost ethereal about her—angelic.

Impulsively, Tara bent forward and lightly flicked one of Marissa's pink nipples with her tongue. Marissa moaned slightly and stirred. Tara closed her lips around the nipple and sucked. Marissa came fully awake and jerked, her expression frightened, her wrists tugging uselessly against the manacles.

"Relax, sweetie. It's only me, Tara. Aaron sent me to let you down. It took me a minute to get used to it, but you look so cute all shorn like a little lamb. You look so adorable, you have no idea. I can actually see your face now, behind all that hair!"

"Oh!" Marissa cried out, completely awake now, remembering with vivid horror how Aaron had cut off all her hair. And she knew Tara was lying, she didn't look sweet, she looked hideous! He'd ruined her! Softly she began to cry, tears streaming down her cheeks, her big brown eyes overflowing.

Tara leaned over her, pressing her own clothed body against the naked and tethered girl. "Oh, don't cry, Marissa. Don't cry. It's only hair. If they cut it off, it was for a good reason. I imagine your pride was getting in the way of your training. It'll grow back. Don't cry." But Marissa continued to cry, turning her head from the other woman.

Sighing, Tara unlocked the cuffs and helped Marissa to step out of the manacles. She held the girl for a moment, massaging the blood back into her cold arms. "You have to put this on," she said. "Aaron's orders. Though what he's thinking, I don't know!" Her face wrinkled with distaste as she held the offending article, with its bright green and orange plaid pattern, printed on polyester that felt stiff as a board compared to the soft cottons and silks the slaves generally wore — when they wore anything at all.

Embarrassed by her shaved pussy, Marissa allowed the housecoat to be placed over her shoulders. She let Tara close the big metal snaps along the front. Marissa wiped her runny nose with the back of her hand. Standing back, Tara grinned at her and said, "You look about ten years old in that thing. Well, come on. You're to meet with Aaron in the exercise room. He wants to inspect you." Leading an exhausted and humiliated Marissa by the hand, together they left the dungeon.

Aaron was sitting in the only chair in the room when Marissa was presented to him by Tara who curtsied and left. Silently he looked over the young woman, at her bald head and her lovely form completely obscured by the bulky housecoat, at least two sizes too large.

He'd expected to find her ugly now, or at least ridiculous. To find her brought down to size, as it were. But instead, his stupid heart lurched at the sight of her tearstained face, the eyes now impossibly big against the closely shaven scalp. Her forehead was high and smooth, and her eyebrows arched prettily, the last reminder of the copper profusion of curls that had so recently adorned her lovely head.

Her collarbone looked as delicate as a bird's, poking above the line of the housecoat. Slender calves emerged from the plaid tent and bare feet, the arches high and delicate. He should leave her in the housecoat—and he would—but for now he gave in to his own desires and said, "Take that off. I'll inspect you now. Assume the inspection position."

Wearily, the sparkle gone from her face, Marissa obeyed, the snaps making a little clicking sound as she pulled open the front of the dress, dropping the stiff garment to the floor. She stood still and straight, arms back, head up and stared at some distant place, her eyes glazed.

Obediently she opened her mouth as he pretended to examine her teeth and tongue. His hands slid down her slender body, feeling for errant hair. He had her lift each foot and looked at her nails and the bottom of her feet. She submitted to all of this without looking at him, without the slightest protest. Had he broken her at last?

Standing in front of her, Aaron cupped her little bare mons, letting his fingers slide over the smooth, pooching little sex. He slipped a finger into the little cleft and into her opening. She wasn't wet! She was dry as a bone and her face was closed, empty of expression. A tiny flame of panic flared inside of him, what had he done?

Was her identity so wrapped up in her appearance that she'd "left the premises", figuratively speaking when he'd cut off the hair that so obviously represented her flashy beauty? Surely she wasn't so shallow? But where had she gone? Where was the spark, the flash of spirit? He had to find her.

"Marissa," he said softly. "Look at me."

Slowly her eyes shifted from the distant point on which they were focused and she seemed to be looking at Aaron's face, perhaps at his mouth. "No. Look into my eyes," he commanded. She obeyed, but her own eyes were flat, as if she was in shock. His heart lurched again. Impulsively he hugged the nude woman to him and lifted her in his arms.

She didn't respond but lay limp against him as he carried her from the room and into her bedroom down the hall. He lay her on the bed and knelt next to her. Knowing he shouldn't do it, but his own desire for once outweighing his good sense and control, he brushed her lips with his own.

They were so soft and they parted slightly against his kiss. His tongue further parted the lips and he felt her respond now, sighing slightly as she began to kiss him back, her long, thin arms encircling his neck, pulling him toward her. They kissed for several moments and the kiss was like hot wine and honey, filling Aaron with a wild ache he knew would never be eased, except with her mouth and those arms holding sweetly around his neck.

When at last he managed to find the inner strength to pull himself away from her, he saw the sparkle had returned. Marissa was awake again, the spirit had only been hiding and it was back. "Oh, Aaron!" she breathed, "I—" But he stopped her words with his fingers against her mouth, his face a warning.

"No!" he said, urgently. "No! Remember who we are. Who I am, who you belong to. Don't speak. I'll let you rest for a while. Dinner will be ready soon and Tara will show you to your new quarters. You're moving down with the house slaves. It's better that way for your training. Now I have to go. Hush, don't say a word." He couldn't let her speak — as it was his control was only holding on by the slimmest thread. She'd break it with a word and then he'd be lost. Quickly he left the room, locking it from the outside as he fled.

Her first night in the dungeon was a strange one. It was almost like being at overnight camp, except instead of giggling campmates, they were all slaves, there by their own desire but living a life of complete submission and servitude. Because she was now "one of them", at least for the time being, the girls talked to her more than they ever had before. Scott stayed away, reading in his own cot, ignoring them all. Marissa was relieved, unaware Aaron had strongly warned Scott to keep his hands to himself and his dick in his pants when around Marissa.

Scott was angry at the restriction — one of his favorite pastimes was sexually abusing the "new meat" as he called the trainees, and Marissa was just about the best-looking one they'd ever had. But his fear of Aaron far outweighed his own horniness. Normally he'd take it out on Anne who was so submissive it was pathetic. He'd fuck her hard and make her display herself for him. But she wasn't even there tonight. André had kept her away somewhere overnight. Theresa had gone home and Diane was sleeping upstairs and thus difficult to get at. Even though she was fat, she was fun to abuse because she was so shy. Oh well, there was always his own hand.

Marissa could see the full moon from the little window set high in the wall. It lit the room with a silvery light. She lay on the cot just beneath Amy who was tossing in the dark, making both beds sway slightly. Marissa had taken off the horrid housecoat, which lay in a heap on the floor by her cot. She was wide-awake, though the lights had been turned out some thirty minutes before, when she heard a whisper, "Marissa, you awake?" It was Tara.

"Yes," she whispered back.

"Can I come over to your cot?"

"Yes," Marissa answered, surprised she had been asked, since they all seemed to take whatever they wanted from her.

Tara slipped quietly from her own cot and lay down next to Marissa. Marissa shifted toward the wall to make room on the narrow bed. "You okay?" Tara asked.

"Yeah, I guess. I can't believe I'm bald but I'm okay, I guess. I can't believe Tom let them do this to me." She turned toward the wall, feeling a prickle of fresh tears against her lids. She waited, expecting a lecture, however well-intentioned from Tara about the sins of pride and virtues of humility, but instead she felt Tara's arms encircle her as she cradled herself against Marissa's curled back.

Marissa was surprised and a little nervous at the thought of another woman so close to her like this. She could feel Tara's breasts pressed against her and the scratchy thistle of her pubic hair. And yet, it was comforting to be held like this when she felt so forlorn. If only it was Aaron's arms around her...

"You're so soft, Marissa. Your skin is so soft." Tara's fingers stroked Marissa's shoulder in smooth circles and Marissa lay still, allowing her to. The circle widened to include Marissa's breast, lightly brushing over the nipple as if accidentally, but always coming back to it. A scene flashed into Marissa's mind from years and years before.

She and her best friend in ninth grade had been giving each other back massages. She had been sleeping over at

Patty's house one weekend. Her friend was straddling Marissa's panty-covered bottom, and Marissa's nightie was pushed up, allowing access to her back.

Patty's fingers had felt so good as they kneaded and soothed the tensions of the day away. And then the fingers had slipped to her sides, caressing for a moment the soft bulge of Marissa's young breasts pressed against the bed. Marissa had shivered with pleasure at the unexpected touch. Then she had stayed very still, to see if it would happen again. It did, and soon the fingers were emboldened and the actual back massage was momentarily forgotten as Patty explored forbidden territory.

When it was Marissa's turn, she straddled her girlfriend's thighs to return the favor. She let her fingers stray down to the sides of Patty's breasts, which even at age fourteen were already large, much larger than Marissa's. Patty sighed at her touch and actually lifted her body slightly, inviting Marissa to reach more of her, to touch all of her breasts. Not a word was spoken between them about what they were doing—not then and not ever—but Marissa still remembered the yielding little marble of Patty's nipple and the feel of it swelling against her fingers as she touched it and finally rolled it between thumb and third finger.

Patty moved away not long after they began this veiled sexual ritual and Marissa had eventually forgotten about her, and the massages, until now. She was still as Tara touched her, more boldly than Patty ever had. Tara's fingers stroked over her body, at once soothing and exciting Marissa. She had never had fantasies about being with another woman but somehow it didn't feel wrong tonight. It felt good.

When Tara pulled at her slightly, indicating she wanted Marissa to turn toward her, Marissa obeyed, responding with her body instead of her mind. Tara hugged her, holding her gently as she lightly kissed Marissa's cheeks, her throat, her eyelids. Finally she risked Marissa's lips and Marissa kissed her back, marveling silently at how soft and sweet her mouth was, so different from a man's.

There was some creaking and rustle as they kissed, but neither one paid much attention, being caught up in their virgin kiss. Suddenly Amy was next to them, crouching on the end of the bed. "Hey you guys, no fair! You're having a party and you didn't invite me!"

Marissa pulled away from Tara abruptly, startled and embarrassed by Amy's sudden presence. She was naked, too, except for the constant silver chastity belt, which was secured as always around her hips.

Marissa felt sorry for her, having to wear that thing, and said so. "Oh, it isn't so bad. I'm used to it, really. I get to come every day anyway, at least once. Either when Michael fucks me or, if he's not in the mood, he likes to have me and Claudette play for his amusement. She can give some excellent head. Oh, my God! That woman has a tongue on her that must be made of gold."

Marissa laughed at the unexpected remark, even though it embarrassed her. She looked shyly at the two women, both so comfortable with their own sexuality. She had always fancied herself as so free and wild, but was coming to realize she was really rather inhibited. It was a surprising admission to herself.

Now Tara gently pressed her back down onto the bed. "Where were we, sweetheart? In a middle of a lovely kiss, if I remember correctly." Gently, she brought her mouth again onto Marissa's and she lay back, letting herself be kissed. It felt so good after such a difficult and strange week.

She was barely aware of it when Amy knelt between her legs and gently pressed apart her thighs. She startled when she felt Amy's warm tongue against her bare, shaven pussy. Her first instinct was to pull away, to sit up and act affronted and ashamed. But her instincts were being overpowered now by Tara's kiss and the soft feather licks of the very skilled and ardent Amy.

Soon she let instincts and thoughts all drift away, like the discarded petals of a flower floating down a little stream. Instead she surrendered to the sheer physical pleasure of being touched and teased. Amy held her legs apart now, licking and tongue-fucking her until she moaned against Tara's mouth still on hers.

Tara dropped down to her nipples, which were erect and eager to receive the gentle bites and kisses offered. Marissa came hard, crying out in pleasure, her cries drowning out Scott's muffled moans as he, too, came—alone on his cot, furiously pumping his cock as he squinted in the silvery dark at the silhouette of the three women performing the fantasy-come-true of so many men.

Marissa actually fell asleep almost as soon as she orgasmed and the two slave girls, smiling indulgently, left her alone, retiring to Tara's cot for more sweet play before they, too, fell asleep, still entangled in each other's arms.

Was it because he was so attracted to her and so angry with himself for that attraction that he planned this day's events? *No*, he told himself. *Don't be ridiculous. You're a professional. Marissa still needs to be taken down a rung or*

three, and you must finish what you started with the shaving.
Today, humiliation is the order of the day.

"Kneel up!" Aaron commanded, as he swept into the bedroom. Marissa had been ordered to report there after breakfast, still dressed in her frumpy housecoat. Frank was behind him, carrying Marissa's toy bag. Marissa who had been sitting on her bed, staring out the window, slid from the bed to the ground and knelt as ordered.

"Gag her. I don't want to hear the whining today." Aaron's voice was low, his emotions tightly controlled. He watched as Frank took the bright red ball gag and held it to Marissa's face.

"Open up," Frank said, grinning at her. Marissa obeyed, her eyes seeking Aaron's, but he wouldn't meet them. Frank secured the little buckles behind Marissa's head, forcing her mouth open wide, tongue pressed back in her mouth so the only sound she could make was a muffled moan.

"Take that thing off her," Aaron said, pointing at her housecoat, and Frank obeyed, standing behind her, leaning over and pulling roughly at the large snaps then pulling the dress from her shoulders and tossing it aside.

"Stand up, Marissa."

As Marissa stood, Frank laughed unkindly and said, "Man, she looks like a plucked chicken with that bald head and that nasty little plucked cunt. Pussies are bad enough without having to see the detail!"

Aaron pursed his lips, as if he was about to speak, but he stopped himself. Let Frank insult her, it would help bring her down from her high throne. Instead he said, "Show him your nasty cunt, slave. Spread it for him. Do it!" The last two words were barked and a startled Marissa slowly dropped her long, lovely fingers to her sex, which she spread slightly, her face burning almost as red as the rubber ball in her mouth.

"Frank's not interested in pussy, certainly not yours! No, we have other plans for you today, Queen Marissa. You're going to be butt-fucked. And you're going to offer your ass to Frank here who might be able to tolerate it, if he closes his eyes and pretends you're just a scrawny young man, right, Frank?"

Frank laughed, rubbing his cock through the fabric of his cotton trousers. "If I close my eyes, maybe I can force myself."

Marissa's eyes widened, and she started to reach back and unbuckle the gag. Perhaps she wanted to speak, but Aaron stopped her, grabbing both her thin wrists in one of his strong hands. "Cuff her, Frank. She still doesn't know how to handle the slightest difficulties. If it isn't about her, and doesn't present her in what she considers her best light, she doesn't want it. Well, too bad, Marissa. Today you don't get a chance to refuse."

What was he doing? Technically, if she needed to speak, he should let her. He should remove the gag, in case she had been going to say she wanted "out" of the contract. This rule of the house had always irritated Aaron, as that little "out" let a slave-in-training know they could always bolt if the going got too tough. And yet, it did happen only very rarely. Most people who "signed up" for this training stayed the duration, unless it turned out they hadn't really come here of their own volition in the first place.

But he realized he didn't want to give Marissa an out anymore. He didn't want to lose these last few precious days. And yet, by the same token, he was determined to break her down, to take away that saucy look in her eye, to dominate that strong will of hers. No, she wouldn't be allowed even a slight chance to get out of it all. Today she would take what he was going to give her, and that was that.

As Frank secured Marissa's wrists behind her back, she made some noises in the back of her throat but, of course, they couldn't understand her words. Aaron led her to the bed and pressed her down against it until she was leaning over it, her cheek resting on the coverlet, her ass at just the right height. Aaron's hand rested firmly against her lower back, keeping her in position.

Even Frank had to admire the high, round ass, the twin globes beautifully muscled and full. "Nice ass," he grudgingly admitted.

"Glad you like it," Aaron dryly reminded him, "because you're going to fuck it."

Marissa started to stand abruptly, but Aaron had anticipated her move and pushed her back down. "No you don't," he said. Quickly he released the clips, which held her cuffs linked together. Nodding at Frank, they each took an arm and stretched them to the chains on the headboard, securing each wrist so that her arms were stretched out on the bed, forcing her to stay bent over at the waist, now immobilized.

Marissa struggled for a moment but she was completely tied down, her mouth stuffed, her body bared and at the mercy of these two men. Tom was miles away and she couldn't even cry out. Aaron leaned over her, his body covering hers. He could feel her heart hammering and her breathing was labored through her nostrils. Her eyes were wide and dark. Aaron's heart actually hurt in his chest.

"Shh, hush now, hush." Aaron put his face next to hers, feeling her impossibly soft skin as he whispered, "I'm here with you. This is what you need, Marissa. This is what your master wants for you. You're not in danger. But you are too proud, little one. You have yet to submit, to truly submit, to anything that wasn't already your idea. I know your shyness about your bottom. This is for your own good, slave girl. You will be anally used, and you will take it, and you will thank me for it. Frank is just my tool. He's a slave, just like you. Do you understand? I want this for you, Marissa. I want you to submit with grace, to accept the humiliation and the pain. To revel in it. Can you do that, Marissa? For me? Can you submit for me?"

He should have said, "for your master, for Tom" but that would have been a lie. He wanted her to submit to *him*. She had penetrated the thick barriers around his heart, God help him. And if he was truly honest, he wanted to be the one to fuck her, to claim her and debase her and by doing so exalt her, but he didn't dare risk it. To fuck her now would be to lose himself to a woman who would be gone by the end of the week.

No, do your job, and keep your stupid feelings out of it, he admonished himself. Smoothing her cheek, he continued to whisper, to calm her, until he felt her yammering heartbeat slow and her breathing ease.

"Yes, angel girl. You can do this. You want to do this for me, don't you?" Slowly Marissa nodded and Aaron felt his heart clutch again, ridiculously. He nodded to Frank who had been standing patiently by, his hand on his cock, making himself hard. At Aaron's nod, Frank dropped his pants and positioned himself behind the tethered girl.

Frank smeared a healthy dollop of lubricant on his cock, the head of which was sizable compared to the rest of it. Poor Marissa would definitely remember this! She looked wildly erotic, with her mouth gagged, her arms extended and chained, her ass displayed, her long, lovely legs spread. Aaron sat next to her, cradling her bare head in his large hands, resisting his impulse to kiss her eyelids.

Marissa's punishment for her natural arrogance would be to be used in a demeaning fashion by a man who had no sexual interest in her whatsoever.

Aaron's punishment for his uncurbed emotions would be to watch.

With a look at Aaron for approval, Frank spread those luscious cheeks and touched his cock head to the tight little rosebud. Marissa jerked, but she couldn't move with her arms chained and Frank's strong hands on either hip holding her still.

Slowly he pressed the head against her asshole, and Marissa squirmed and squealed into her gag. "This part hurts the worst," Aaron said. "Show me how brave you are, slave girl. How submissive. Take it, for me." And Marissa stilled, though, sitting next to her on the bed, his hand on her back, he could feel her heart pounding again. Her eyes squeezed tightly shut as Frank continued to push, gently but surely, not backing off.

Frank held her cheeks apart, which served to prevent her from clenching her muscles, and actually made it much less painful than if he had just entered her as she tensed against him. Still, she was so tight and he groaned, loving the feel of the tight ass massaging his cock. As André's slave, he was usually on the receiving end of this treatment, and savored the chance now offered.

Marissa struggled against him as he pushed himself fully into her. In and out he moved, his cock slick with lubricant. If Frank was embarrassed to be fucking this girl in the ass in front of the trainer, it didn't show. His head dropped back, his eyes closed, his fingers kneading the flesh of her ass as he fucked her, alternating the tempo, getting her used to the onslaught.

She stilled somewhat and Aaron saw Frank's cock was fully buried to the hilt. He moved slowly, easing himself almost out of her body and then he suddenly slammed into her, forcing Marissa's body forward as she screamed against the ball gag.

Aaron shot a warning look at Frank who grinned sheepishly and settled back to a regular rhythm. Marissa moaned against her gag and Aaron reached out impulsively, stroking her face. Her eyes opened and she stared straight into his, her expression imploring.

Knowing he shouldn't do it, knowing he wouldn't do it if this was just another novice-in-training, Aaron reached behind her head and unbuckled the little clasps that held the ball gag in place.

"Oh!" Marissa breathed. "Thank you! Thank you for taking it off!" She worked her jaw, opening and closing her mouth. She couldn't touch her own face as she was still bound to the bed and Frank still stood bent over her, his cock in her bottom. Aaron watched her closely as Frank used her body, increasing his tempo as he neared his own release. With each thrust she jerked forward, and now was able to gasp aloud, but she wasn't crying, and she wasn't begging Frank to stop or Aaron to release her.

Instead her eyes were locked onto Aaron's. She couldn't seem to remember his rule that she not stare into his face, and for some reason he didn't admonish her. Instead he focused on those lips and on not bending over to kiss them. As if reading his mind, she pouted, her lips red and full, pursed as if waiting for his kiss. As if he was her lover, not her trainer.

Oh, those eyes—they pulled him into her, made him want to lose himself. He saw the flash of will. She wasn't subdued at all by what was happening to her, she was ignited! The woman was no more submissive than he was! She was a masochist, pure and simple. A little slut who loved the fight but only obeyed under duress. He shouldn't be wasting another minute of his time on her! He should leave her to the house slaves or give her to André. Yes, André would literally whip her into shape. He wouldn't be moved by her impossible beauty, by her yearning looks and sweet appeals. He would cane her 'til she passed out, and she would deserve it!

Aaron himself did not favor the cane, it was too brutal for his taste and often cut the flesh, even when carefully wielded. Which wasn't to say he didn't wield it with skill, but that was his job, not his preference. He preferred the buoyant smack of the crop or thuddy lush strokes of a heavy flogger. The image of Marissa chained in the exercise room came back to him. He saw her stretched taut, the sweat a shimmer on her bare body, her head back, copper hair on fire in the suffused light, her spirit dancing on the edge of that whipping as she flew into that sexual perfection where pain and pleasure melted together, fusing the master and slave as surely as any sexual act. It was as if his hand, holding the whip, became part of her body, experiencing each lash as she did—the sting, the kiss, the melting into pleasure, the pure surrender...

Abruptly Aaron stood up and Marissa's eyes followed him, but she was immobilized. "That's enough, Frank. We're done today." Frank, completely unaware of the strange dynamic in the room, thrust forward several more times, shooting his hot load deep into Marissa's ass, making her scream with the last brutal thrusts of his own pleasure. Pulling out, he wiped himself with a towel ready for the purpose and pulled his pants on, smiling hugely with satisfaction.

"I said we're done. Get out." Aaron said, afraid to examine his building rage that he had allowed, indeed ordered, this callous house slave to defile Marissa in this way. She was laying still, her cheek resting against the soft quilts, no doubt waiting for Aaron to release her.

And he longed to, but not to continue any lesson. He wanted to gently wash her, and then cradle her in his arms and whisper all the secrets of his heart to her. Aaron, master of self-control, no longer knew why he was there or what his own motives were. Willing himself to ignore the still-bound young woman bent naked and spread against the bed, he went out into the hall, using the little house phone to call Claudette. Let her clean up the girl, he was done.

Tom woke up suddenly, alone in his big bed overlooking Central Park. The angle of the sun told him he had slept later than he had intended. Shifting onto his back, he put his hands behind his head, staring at the ceiling, the net of his dreams still lingering over him. Marissa was due to come home in a few days. But it wasn't Marissa he had been dreaming about. It was Anne, and his cock was rock-hard with the memory, rising like a tent pole under the soft sheets.

Throwing back the covers, he ignored his erection, going into the marble master bathroom for his shower and shave. Today, instead of meeting with Strata InfoSystems president Bill Woods as previously scheduled, he was going to meet with André and Anne, and have another "lesson".

He found André somewhat pompous, but when he was able to focus on what the man was saying, he really did have some rather sound advice it seemed to Tom. Tom had asked and André had agreed to allow Anne to join them for breakfast first, before they all went down to the club dungeon for more "hands-on" experience.

Tom felt like he was going out on a first date in high school as he tried on first one outfit and then another. Finally he settled on a pale cream cashmere sweater and black jeans. Who was he trying to impress? He didn't answer his own question but hurried out the door.

Tom arrived at the little café where they had agreed to meet. He was generally about five minutes early wherever he went, punctuality being something of an obsession of his. So he was able to watch as André and Anne came around the corner from the hotel where they were staying. They looked like a father and grown daughter walking together, André's hand proprietarily on Anne's elbow. Anne was beautifully dressed, not in the little silk thing she had been wearing at the castle, but in a dark royal blue suit, the jacket long and the skirt short and cut close against very sexy legs. Even though she was petite, she was muscular and slim in a very feminine way.

Her heels were quite high, easily five inches, which made her almost as tall as André. If they were difficult to walk in, she certainly didn't show it, almost gliding along the sidewalk. Her buttermilk blonde hair was pulled back in an elegant French braid and she looked like a model or young executive on her way to a business meeting.

Well, this was business, wasn't it? Though it was certainly pleasurable! Tom smiled, extending his hand to

André as they approached. "Hello, Anne," he said, turning toward her and she responded with a nod and a murmur, smiling shyly.

Once they were seated and orders taken, André got down to business. "I thought we'd work on a few positions today. I'll teach you what Aaron has been teaching Marissa so you can use the terminology to some effect.

"I will also demonstrate some very effective tortures for the misbehaving slave. There are some wonderful pieces of equipment down there in the dungeon, you know. And I've made sure we will have the place to ourselves so we won't be disturbed."

The food arrived, eggs and sausage for the men, blueberry blintzes for Anne, whose eyes lit up when they were placed before her. After André took several bites he said, "There were a few things I wanted to discuss yesterday with you and we didn't get a chance. Aaron tells me Marissa is highly sexual and seems to be used to getting what she wants when she wants it."

Tom felt he was supposed to defend himself at that moment, but as he started to speak André held up a hand, smiling. "Please, I do not intend this as a criticism. She is your lover and before she came to us, your untrained lover. And don't misunderstand me. Interaction with a slave girl can be intimate and caring, but it is not based on equality or reciprocity of action. When you get her home, establish this with your slave from the beginning. Make certain she understands her sexual release is no longer a 'right' but a privilege, and it comes to her not for *her* benefit but for *your* pleasure.

"It's also important to know your slave. Though she will be trained to some degree when you get her back,

Marissa will still have a long way to go, and it's up to you to teach her and continue to train her to suit your desires. But it is very important you know her limits and needs when punishment is involved. Not all punishments work for all slaves. Punishments that involve pain should be thoughtfully executed—a slave should know she's being punished, but should never be given more pain than she can handle. Punishments that involve isolation or ignoring your slave should be executed just as thoughtfully.

"Do not overuse punishment. If you do, you run the risk of a slave whose obedience is based on fear rather than the genuine desire to serve. A slave should not obey because she fears punishment but because her true desire is to make you happy. On the other hand, punishment should not be pleasurable, and the slave should understand the consequences of disobedience will be either painful or stressful in another way.

"Anne here is almost never punished. She is so eager to serve and to please that she rarely requires correction." Anne blushed and looked down at her plate, though a small smile hovered on her lips. "Which isn't to say, of course, that she isn't regularly tortured and abused. But that's for our pleasure and, incidentally, for hers."

Once in the dungeon, Anne was instructed to remove her clothing and kneel, dressed only in stockings, garters and high heels, to await the men's pleasure. Tom couldn't help but stare, though André seemed completely indifferent to her charms. Tom noted her bottom was still marked with a pale purple crisscross of faded welts, wrought by his own hand yesterday. He controlled his desire to touch them, to smooth the skin he had abraded the day before.

André discoursed on the various standard slave positions, which Anne demonstrated with grace and precision. Tom wondered if he should be taking notes. He realized he didn't really go in for all this formality but he did enjoy watching Anne kneeling, spreading her legs, exposing her sex, bending and swaying in various complicated moves, like some X-rated ballerina without a trace of self-consciousness.

Next they moved to the instruments of torture. "I wanted to show you some clever things you can do at home, since we don't always have a place like the dungeon available." The first one, called "the pony" was basically a wooden bar set on two sturdy tripods, much like a construction sawhorse. It was a nice smooth piece of wood about two inches thick with a half-inch flat surface. The tripods were adjustable, depending on the height of the subject and the intensity of the torture.

André had Anne straddle the pony. "Sometimes you will just bind the slave's hands behind her back but since we have this nice setup here, I'm going to secure them to the ceiling, like so." Taking Anne's offered wrists, already cuffed in dark blue leather that matched her garters and heels, he secured them to dangling chains and then ratcheted the chains until Anne was standing on tiptoe, her legs shapely in their high heels on either side of the bar.

"Next," he explained as he worked, "we raise the bar like so, until it is resting snugly under the slave. It's adjusted so as to offer the subject a choice — stand on tiptoe or rest the calf muscles and bear her weight on her pussy. As she tires, she will spend more time with her weight on that most sensitive region. The higher the pony is set the shorter the time required to bring her to an exquisite agony." For the moment, Anne was still on her toes, calf muscles flexed, her pussy spared.

"Anne's strong," André noted. "She can stay on tiptoe quite a while. But eventually she won't be able to stay up and her pussy will take the punishment." Tom watched her for a moment, wondering how far André was going to take this.

But André was already moving on. "Let her down, will you? I'm sorry I don't have an assistant today, but it will be good practice anyway for you." André watched as Tom released Anne's cuffs from the chains and helped her off the pony. "You can build a pony at home easily with a piece of wood and two camera tripods, as you can see."

As Tom released Anne from her bonds, he caught her scent, something delicate and floral. He resisted an impulse to smell her hair, to touch her face. André, now completely unaware of the two of them, was busy removing several long strands of sturdy-looking rope from his bag of toys.

"Another handy torture is what I call the kneeling stress torture. It's extremely effective, albeit a bit tricky to set up. The idea is to bind the slave in such a way that kneeling up on the knees is impossible and at the same time kneeling down on the haunches is equally impossible. Come, Anne."

Anne knelt obediently while André executed a number of skillful knots around her thighs, forcing her into an awkward position, which looked quite uncomfortable to Tom. Of course, that was the point. "This treatment can easily run over an hour before Anne begs for mercy. Scott will whine after just thirty minutes. I enjoy watching them struggle to balance. Frank will fall over and, of course, I have to whip him then, that bad boy."

André smiled fondly, clearly seeing his lover in his mind's eye.

Once he had untied Anne, André said, "Now, perhaps you would like another round with the cane?" He brought out the same cane, this time saying, "I would like to present this one to you as a gift. You seemed to have a natural affinity for it yesterday." He bowed slightly, smiling graciously.

Tom took the cane and flexed it between both hands. He did want to whip Anne, but he didn't want to do it in front of André. He wanted something more private, more — intimate.

Tom realized suddenly this was probably the last time he'd ever see Anne. And he realized he couldn't bear the thought! How could it be that he'd fallen in love with her when they'd barely exchanged a word between them? And what about Marissa who was waiting for him back at Le Chateau, expecting to be taken back into his arms and his heart? Guilt overwhelmed him while at the same time his practical mind reminded him he didn't really know Marissa much better than he knew Anne. She had entered his life on a whirlwind of romance, but there was no particular history. No real loyalty beyond sexual attraction and vague yearnings.

He'd make it up to Marissa. He'd give her some money. In his heart of hearts he knew that was what she really wanted anyway. He'd give her a "gift" of an investment portfolio and give her some leads in whatever field she might be interested in pursuing.

Tom realized with a start he'd been standing there for several moments while André and Anne waited patiently for his response. Did he want to cane poor little Anne?

Forcing his mind to the issue at hand, Tom made a sudden decision.

"No, André. Thank you. I don't want to whip Anne right now, though I appreciate the gift of this lovely cane. I'll tell you what I do want." His voice was confident now, the voice he used when he'd made a sound business decision and had the means to move on it. "I want to know if Anne is still—" he hesitated then plunged on, "—for sale. Both you and Claudette mentioned before she was— to the right person, for the right price. I'd like to know more about it."

Anne gasped, the first sound she'd made since thanking the waitress for her food. Tom glanced at her quickly, afraid he would see disgust or fear on her face at the thought of leaving her place as "house slave" to come and live with him. But what he saw gave him even greater courage and resolve.

She had been looking down as he spoke. Time seemed to slow to a stop. He found he was drawn to her as one is drawn to a solitary light in a room. Whether one wills it or not, it becomes the focus. His heart pounded in his head and chest as he waited, forgetting to breathe.

She looked up, straight at Tom, her face smooth, her eyes clear and frank. He saw her features soften into a lovely smile, her eyes fairly shining and he started to breathe again as time resumed its normal path and the world clicked on again.

André may have been surprised, but if so, he concealed it completely, only replying, "Yes, she is indeed for sale. But, of course, the sale must be consensual. Anne would have to consent, and terms would need to be agreed upon. And then, of course, there is the small matter of Marissa."

Marissa. Yes, the small matter of Marissa. He would dwell on that later. For now, Anne dressed and they left The Club. It was lunchtime and they would talk over food and wine. Even the guilt over Marissa couldn't quell the little swift, singing happiness, very small, very bright, inside of him.

Chapter Eleven

"He *what*?" Marissa still couldn't process what she was hearing, though Michael had repeated it to her several times already.

Patiently he said yet again, "He has decided to give up his status as your owner, Marissa. He's releasing you from the contract and all that it implies." Michael pushed a small box over the desk toward Marissa. It contained her purse and some of her jewelry. "Tom say's he'll mail the rest of the things you left at his house by the end of the week."

Marissa felt stunned, and like she was going to be sick. "He's dumping me! That's what you're saying with all that fancy language, aren't you! He's dumping me! First, he has Aaron cut off my hair!" As she spoke, her hand flew to her still bare scalp. "Then he says, oh well, I'm tired of Marissa now. She can go to hell!" Marissa burst into tears, doubling over in her chair across the desk from Michael, her face hidden in her hands.

"That's not entirely true, actually. He has given me a rather sizable investment portfolio in your name, for when you leave here. All you have to do is sign some documents, and you can continue with the investments or liquidate them. He's actually left you rather well off, in the circumstances."

Marissa peeked through her fingers to see if Michael was serious. Tom had left her money? Guilt money. Blood money as he betrayed her! She started to cry again, though the cool, clinical part of her brain had filed away the knowledge that at least she wasn't destitute.

Michael rose and came to sit next to her. "Shh, hush, sweetheart. It's not the end of the world. He was your lover, you know, nothing more. You weren't married. You only knew one another a short time, am I right? Did you love him? Tell me honestly, Marissa. Did you love Tom with enough passion and devotion to serve him as his willing and submissive slave girl?"

Marissa continued to cry, but she was listening, and even through her tears, through the shame of rejection, she knew he was right. She hadn't loved Tom and now she saw he hadn't loved her either. She had been depending on him to "save" her, to provide her a luxurious home and "the easy life", basically in return for her services as a sex slave.

It had sounded exotic and this two-week stint wasn't too much to endure to get the life of ease she planned on securing through Tom. Love really hadn't entered the equation.

And, if she was totally honest, there was a tiny flame of hope surging up through the ashes of her despair. A little phoenix of hope spreading its wings inside of her. If she was free...available, would he—oh, she didn't even dare think his name—would he, possibly, want her? Not as a slave-in-training, but for his own?

She took the tissues Michael offered, blowing her nose noisily and wiping her eyes. She was still wearing the ridiculous housecoat Aaron had forced on her and she looked like a little child, wiping her nose, her feet curled under her in the big yellow leather chair.

"Do you have somewhere to go?" Michael asked kindly.

"Not really," Marissa answered truthfully. She hadn't paid her share of the rent at her apartment, and if she knew her roommates, her room was already sublet, and whatever they hadn't divvied up between them was in a box somewhere in the hallway or in the dump, if someone hadn't stolen it.

"You may stay here, if you like. If you think you have what it takes to be a house slave. It takes a particular kind of dedication. You have to be willing to be used, sexually and otherwise, by any and every person here, even the other slaves. You would live basically as you are living now, but you would be required to contribute to the household in some fashion. That could be worked out. We would put money aside for you, in an account, for when you were ready to return to 'the real world'."

Marissa looked at him, weighing the possibility in her mind. It sounded absurd on its face. Marissa Winston a house slave? And yet, as she thought of Anne, and Tara and Amy, and even Frank and Scott—they all seemed so contented with their "lot", so at ease in their own skins. Was this something she could do?

"Would I have to sign something? Another stupid contract?"

Michael smiled at her insolence. This one was not submissive, he could see that clearly. And yet she had made real progress in her training, and there was no doubt she was beautiful, even without her long, shiny hair. He liked her spunk and her spirit. And it would be a pleasure punishing her when she got out of line, which he imagined would be frequently.

"No. House slaves have no formal contract. At any time you could be asked to leave, or you could leave on your own. No strings."

"Do…do slaves often get asked to leave?"

"No. The ones we choose generally stay until they are ready to go or someone buys them. We're quite selective, you know. I didn't make the offer lightly."

"Buys them? For real?"

"As real as anything, I suppose. You create your own sales contract, with our help, of course. You fix a price. It isn't always monetary. Sometimes it's just a list of expectations, if you like, of requirements, limits. And then, of course, they can't just waltz in and buy you like they would a horse or a pet puppy. It's a consensual thing, and you have the final say."

He paused, and then added, almost casually, "Anne has just been purchased, by the way. She won't be here anymore. She left today."

"Anne!" Marissa sat up, startled by this new information into forgetting her own predicament, if just for a moment. Marissa pictured the petite blonde, kneeling naked and obedient. She remembered her kindness that first night when Marissa had been forced to eat on the floor. "Anne was 'bought'? She's gone? Well, who bought her? Where'd she go?" Marissa realized she hadn't seen Anne for the last several days. It was almost as if Anne had been avoiding her.

But Michael was shaking his head. "I'm sorry, Marissa. That's confidential. We would never reveal that sort of information to anyone who didn't have an express right to know it."

"Huh," said Marissa, contemplatively. She sat up, smoothing the polyester smock against her thighs. Her face was still puffy, eyes reddened from her tears, but on the whole she seemed to be bearing up rather well. "Can I have time to think about this house slave thing? I have a lot to think about."

"Of course. Take all the time you need."

It had been three days. Silently she waited, hope dovetailing despair, neither quite winning out. Marissa helped in the kitchen, cutting vegetables, mixing batters, washing down counters. She also helped Tara with laundry and dusting. Nothing much. She hadn't made a decision yet, to go or to stay, and no one had pressed her, though Tara and Amy had eagerly begged her to stay. She was waiting for something. For someone.

Aaron had disappeared the day after Michael had made Tom's decision known to her. Marissa's training, which only had two days to go, was cut short when Tom released her from the contract. And so Aaron must have known what had happened.

At first Marissa had waited eagerly for him to come to her. In her mind, or not quite in it yet, but lurking on the edges, was the idea he would throw over everything, stride in and sweep her off her feet. She spent her whole first day after Tom's rejection in a state of nervous anxiety, not allowing the hope that was coiled inside of her to furl open, not yet.

But when he didn't come, nor send for her at all that first day or the next, she deflated. Tara found her crying quietly on her cot when she was supposed to be peeling potatoes for the evening's soup. Tara didn't ask what the matter was, she assumed it was Tom's abandonment that had left her in tears. She stroked Marissa's soft, fuzzy head, and murmured, "There, dear. It'll be fine, you know. He obviously wasn't worth it, the coward. Just leaving you here without even an explanation."

"No," Marissa managed, between sobs. "I don't care about him. He was a meal ticket. It's...it's—" she felt stupid suddenly, admitting she had this ridiculous crush—oh, so much more than a crush—on her trainer, on the man who found constant fault with her every little move.

"What, honey? It isn't your owner? What in the world has you in tears? Did Scott mess with you again? Just laugh at him, that's what we all do, except Anne. That is, when she was here." Tara paused, looking away suddenly, the pieces of a puzzle suddenly clicking into place. She knew, though Marissa didn't, where Anne had been taken those two days before she had returned to collect her things. She guessed now where Anne had gone.

Turning toward Marissa again, she said, her voice falsely bright, "See, she got sold, maybe you will, too! If that's what you want, I mean."

Marissa looked at her, and shook her head. "No. I don't want to be sold! I want, oh, God, I can't believe I'm admitting this, but I want," her voice dropped to a whisper, "I want Aaron."

Tara forgot about Anne and the secret intrigues with Tom. Aaron! Cold, unreachable, implacable Aaron. Unlike Michael and André who regularly used and abused the house slaves, Aaron almost never partook, though he had every right. When he wasn't training, he was in his private quarters, doing God knew what. Or he was gone. The girls always wished he would use them, as he was so good-looking and so sexy.

Early on they had speculated he might be gay, but decided even if he was that wouldn't explain his aloofness since André and Frank were gay and they certainly made use of whoever they wanted whenever they wanted!

"Oh, Marissa," Tara said, looking worried. "You can forget that one. He's made of ice, except his heart, which is solid stone."

But Marissa remembered the kiss. Did she imagine it? No, it had happened and there had been sweetness in it and fire, and it wasn't just her own passion that had ignited it. Was it? Was she that delusional, thinking every man wanted her, only to find that none of them really did? Not Tom, not Aaron? If only she could see him again! Explain about Tom, and how she didn't care and only wanted him, wanted Aaron, under any terms, any at all, even as his part-time, house-slave slut.

"And anyway, he isn't here," Tara added.

"What do you mean, he isn't here?"

"Just what I said. He left town for a few days. That's what he told Claudette, anyway, who told me. Wants to 'get his head straight' about something, I think she said." At Marissa's stricken expression she added, "He'll be back. Couple of days. He has a new slave to train, anyway. A young woman from France, I hear. Doesn't even speak English, but some things are universal, I guess."

Another slave! A beautiful, young European seductress with lots of hair on her head! Marissa touched her bald pate, feeling the peach fuzz, tears slipping over again. Tara said, "You got it bad, girl! Get over it! He is so off-limits it's stupid! And anyway, you probably aren't in love with him. Lots of people think they love their trainer, but they just love what the trainer does, what he represents. That whole control thing and exchange of power. You can confuse that with love, you know. Lots of people do. You'll get over him in no time. I did." She grinned conspiratorially.

Marissa, not used to wearing her heart on her sleeve, especially not in front of another woman, nodded and tried to smile, wiping her eyes with her fingers. She smoothed the soft fabric of her dress, unconsciously bunching the hem between her fingers for comfort. At least she wasn't wearing the nasty polyester outfit anymore. It had been stuffed into the trash can as soon as she was informed her formal training was over. She was given two soft shifts, one in pale blue cotton and one in soft black silk.

Today she was in the black silk—she loved the way it draped seductively over her body, making her feel feminine and alluring. If only Aaron could see her in it, instead of that horrible plaid thing he'd had her wear...

Aaron sat still, looking out his large bay window, not seeing the deep green of the pines as the bright light fractured and sequined on the moving water of the small lake in his view. The setting sun made the air look buttery and golden. But the beauty was lost on Aaron, whose thoughts were miles away.

Or a few floors away. He saw her as if she was sitting next to him or kneeling at his feet. It was a sensitive, dreamy face, lit by the most magnificent dark eyes. Aaron, unbeknownst to any of the slave staff, was locked away in the private part of the house, which was his own. Normally he loved sitting in his small study, lined with books, all of which were dear to his heart and had been read many times each.

A little calico cat curled itself around his legs, purring gently. It hopped up onto his knees and wound itself into a knot, face hidden, and fell asleep instantly. Absently his hands found the cat's warm little body and he stroked it softly, comforting himself as much as pleasing the animal.

Aaron had always prided himself on his ability to keep his work and play separate. He was a man who had held himself back for so long that his body and his heart had forgotten what it was to yield, to give oneself to another, to trust. He knew his appeal to women, and had always kept himself in careful check for precisely that reason. He knew because of his position as trainer, he had a unique potential to abuse his station. When a woman submitted to him, truly gave of herself, she invariably felt such a strong connection to him that just a flick of his finger, a push to her heart and he knew he could claim her.

He knew Marissa was there now, ready to fall to his perceived charms, which probably had little to do with himself and everything to do with his position. And he had led her on with that kiss. Oh, that kiss! How he wanted her! But he didn't want her on those terms. He didn't want a woman he had basically tricked into wanting him, not because he was Aaron, but because he was the one in command, the one who gave her what she craved.

The plot had thickened now with Mr. Reed's surprising rejection of the sparkling Marissa for the quiet grace of Anne. Aaron was aware of Anne's appeal and she was, without doubt, beautifully trained. While understood intellectually how a man might prefer such a "true" submissive as Anne, he himself would never have considered her as a lover.

So why was he sitting here moping? Marissa, the girl he knew was strictly off-limits these past weeks as he explored, molded and directed her, was suddenly "free". The girl-on-loan was even now unclaimed, a temporary house slave, apparently mulling her own fate over as she helped with chores and played with the other girls.

Aaron smiled, imagining Tara and Amy, and how they wouldn't be able to keep their hands off Marissa. How would she handle that girl-girl dynamic? He sensed she was very much used to being with men, and fully aware of her power over them. But when faced with other women, both of whom were lovely in their own right, how would she cope? Was she open enough, confident enough, to find out how sweet the kiss of another woman could be?

Marissa. When they had kissed and he had pulled away, he saw the yearning in her face. She was no master of her emotions, as he was. She was ripe for claiming, now especially, surely on the rebound of a rejection. Aaron was reasonably sure she had never loved Tom, but that wouldn't have stopped the barb of abandonment from piercing her pride, wounding her girlish heart.

His mind drifted and he felt himself plucking, pulling, at the scar tissue over his own wound that had never completely healed. So many years ago, they were both children really, he barely twenty, she nineteen. Head over heels, stupid in love. Running off despite their parents' combined rage, marrying secretly, swearing each other was all they needed, would ever need. How he had believed that!

Julia. Her face no longer haunted his dreams, but the loss of her had sealed his heart, he had thought for good. Julia, in the arms of another, Julia, her face a mask of horror when she turned, in slow motion, naked on her knees, another man's cock buried in her from behind. Aaron home early, so excited about some stupid thing he no longer remembered now.

He would have forgiven her, was already on the way to forgiving her, even as he felt his heart cracking, a sharp thwack that was actually physical in its intensity. But she told him, over many tears and cups of tea, that her heart belonged to another. He had begged and groveled, completely humiliated and ashamed of his own need. But she was steadfast, impervious, finally cold in the face of his pleading. She divorced him and disappeared from his life so completely he no longer knew if she was even alive. She took a piece of him with her, ripped out a part of him that he never thought would grow back.

Aaron grew up after that, he supposed. He would never again be that vulnerable, that dependent on a woman. There had been that one "slip up" with Elena, but he'd caught himself in time. Never again. He had had many affairs since then, but none were of the heart. And this suited him. It was safe, it was fun, it was easy. Really, this setup now was ideal, wasn't it? Marissa was now fair game. He could take her on a little tour of Europe. Impress her with his continental flair. Use her completely — use her up and then, *au revoir, ma petite. C'est la vie, nous sommes finis.*

He could have Marissa if he wanted, he was certain. He could make the conquest, claim the girl and ride off into the sunset. Except for the small fact it would compromise everything he held dear. Except for the fact he would feel like a fraud. For Aaron, the essence of strength was not in overpowering others but in mastering oneself. Love is giving, as well as receiving, and when one has once known love, one sees conquest as the act of a weak and selfish person, the momentary satisfaction of an appetite. As the sun set completely, he turned from the window, his face obscured in shadow.

Michael handed Marissa the papers. "It's all here. You just need to sign it. Claudette is a notary, she'll take care of it for you. You've got quite a tidy little portfolio there. It's valued at over one hundred thousand on paper. It's all quite liquid, too. I had my attorney review it for you, to make sure there was nothing 'funny' about it, but it's quite aboveboard. You must have made quite an impression on Mr. Reed."

"Yeah, so much of an impression that he dumped me and left me here." Marissa's expression was bitter, but Michael saw the sadness beneath it, the loss.

"I shouldn't speak out of turn. This is none of my affair, but I like you, Marissa. I want to be frank with you, if you'd like my opinion." He waited, crossing his fingers over his substantial girth, his eyes kind.

Marissa said, "Sure, I'd love to hear it." Her voice was flat.

"Tom and you were not suited. No, hear me out. I had an opportunity to observe him at close hand, as did André. You could never have given him what he wanted. He needs someone who is completely submissive, subservient to his needs and desires. We could have trained you to behave as if you were submissive. You could have learned to bend and yield with grace and utterly convincing charm. But Marissa, I truly believe it would have been an act for you, a charade. A game to get what you wanted or believed you wanted.

"At the risk of offending, what a hollow life for both of you. If you are there because your heart demands it or your sexual needs beg for it, I understand. But just to secure a safe haven or creature comforts? What's the point? Life is too short to just give it away for a comfortable bed and a maid."

Marissa stared at him, knowing she should be offended but her defenses were rubbed raw enough not to bother any longer. She blurted, "God, it's true. It is. I feel so stupid and embarrassed to have been dumped, and be sitting here like an ugly little duck with no hair and no life!" Her eyes filled with tears as she felt her shame, but she plunged on. "But you're right! What was it all really, but pride and a desire to be taken care of? Well, he did end up doing that, didn't he? I can get along on that money. I've always wanted to go to college, you know? I could do that now, if I want. I could live carefully, and go to school and get a degree. I could do that!" She smiled at Michael, her face lighting up for a second then clouding, shutting down as if a candle had been blown out.

"What is it, dear?" Michael asked quietly.

Marissa mumbled and Michael said, "Speak up. I can't understand you."

"Nothing," she said. "Just a stupid girl thing. Forget it."

He nodded, respecting her right to private thoughts, though he could see they saddened her. "So I assume you won't be staying on with us?" The image of her lovely, naked body when he'd had the pleasure of strapping her round, perfect bottom came unbidden to him, but he pushed it away, there would be many other lovely girls to use and torture.

Marissa smiled, but agreed, "I guess I'm just not cut out for the life of a slave girl, huh? I'll miss the girls but between us, I won't miss Scott!" *I will miss Aaron*, she thought, but the words remained unspoken. Then, she dared, "I heard Aaron was out of town? England?"

"Where'd you hear that? No, he's here. Just taking a little rest in his quarters. His new charge will be here tomorrow. He likes to meditate between assignments, keep himself fresh."

He's here. The words resonated in her head like a bell tolling a death knell. *He's here.* She'd been "free" for three days, waiting, yearning, hope clinging like a shroud for the moment when he'd return. But he was here. Could he have been any clearer? Whatever silly dreams she'd attached to that kiss were just that. Slowly Marissa stood, extending her hand to Michael. He saw the price she paid for her composure and, though not knowing the source of the pain, admired her for it.

"It's perfect. I'll take it." Marissa twirled around the tiny apartment. It was little more than a room with a tiny bathroom and little alcove that held a stove and half-size refrigerator, but it was in the Village, just north of Washington Square, right near NYU, where Marissa was going to start classes in September, and, most importantly, it was within her budget.

After her head had cleared some, she realized she probably shouldn't take all the money Tom had "bequeathed" to her. It was crazy to accept a "gift" of that size, and anyway, there were probably strings attached. Though accepting it would mean the end to the realization of any immediate dreams, she'd made an effort to return the money to Tom. The "old" Marissa would never have even thought of doing that, she'd have taken the money and run.

But something had changed. Marissa no longer wanted to get by on her looks or her ability to manipulate a man. The hint of a possibility that there could be more had somehow begun a fledgling shift in Marissa's character. And she was trying to find a way to accept that even though she would never see Aaron again, she had tasted a moment of something that made her realize there was more to life than she'd imagined.

Marissa had called Tom and he had agreed to meet her at a bistro, once she had assured him it wasn't "about them" and that she was "over it", which was true. They had both had been shy and embarrassed. Though saying nothing of his current circumstance, Tom tried to explain himself and to apologize for his misplaced affections, but Marissa had cut him off, admitting she herself had been less than honest with him and with herself.

He'd convinced her to keep the investments as a gift, as a salve, really, for his own guilt, though he didn't say that. He assured her there were no further obligations and he'd be honored if she'd accept the money as a token of his remaining affection for her. They'd parted as friends, airily promising to keep in touch, though both knew they wouldn't.

"Aaron, we'll miss you more that I can say, but I respect your decision. And I know you've volunteered to stay and do this final slave training since you'd committed to it prior. But really it isn't necessary. To tell you the truth, I've been getting a bit bored myself lately. I'm rather looking forward to training the little Dominique myself. From what I gather, she's something of a wild child, not unlike the recently departed Marissa."

Michael and Aaron were sitting in Michael's study, each in a large yellow chair, Michael relaxed, Aaron perched tensely on the edge of his chair. At the mention of Marissa he involuntarily drew in his breath and turned away, but not before Michael had seen the pain in his face.

Suddenly he understood. Marissa's sadness beneath her resolve to strike out on her own, and Aaron's unexpected decision to quit the training business—or take a leave of absence, as he'd called it.

They were in love! But did they realize it? He smiled and casually inquired, "Have you kept in touch with Ms. Winston? I have her new address, you know."

"Me? No. No, why would I do that?"

"Why indeed?" Michael mused, but left the man to his private thoughts, thinking of his own Claudette and how joyously lucky he was to have her.

Marissa was bent over her papers, biting the end of her pen, trying to finish her art history essay on *Fin de Siècle* Impressionism. Maybe it wasn't a practical major, like accounting or teaching, but it drew her interest. She had always loved color and texture, and though she didn't think she had much artistic talent herself, she knew what she liked, and enjoyed learning about the history of the pictures she had admired for so long in New York's many and varied museums. And she figured she could find work in a museum or library once she was done with her degree. She would follow her heart for once, and the money—or lack of it—be damned!

For the first time in her adult life, she wasn't depending on a man for her happiness. Oh, she missed him horribly, and hadn't yet let go of secret dreams, but she realized she didn't have to have him and life would go on, and eventually maybe even be good. She wouldn't exactly call herself happy, but she felt competent and excited to be attending university.

The buzzer sounded, persistent and ugly like an angry hornet 'til she dropped her pen and said aloud, "Now who could that be?" She wasn't expecting anyone. Hardly anyone even knew where she lived now as she'd dropped out of the chic party scene completely and hadn't kept up with her so-called friends.

Stepping to the little intercom she pressed the button and said, "Yes?"

"Marissa?"

That voice. Her heart stopped at its sound. It had been thirty-two days since she'd last seen him, last heard that resonant lovely tone, the pure rich vowels of his perfect British diction. That tiny secret dream she'd pressed down flat beneath her heart bloomed into a blazing flower.

She realized she hadn't responded and managed, "Yes?"

"It's Aaron. Aaron Sterling." Aaron Sterling. What a lovely name, sterling silver. Pure and perfect. What was he doing here?

Pressing the button to release the lock downstairs, she said, trying to sound calm and casual, "Please, come on up. It's number seven." She hoped he could hear her, because she could barely hear herself over the roaring of her blood in her ears.

She glanced at herself in the mirror, hands rising from the habit of years, to push back her shiny, thick hair. She grinned ruefully at her chick-fuzz head and then bit her lips and slapped her cheeks—no time for makeup, he was on the way up!

When she opened the door, he was just raising his knuckles to rap on it and they both laughed. She'd forgotten how tall he was! He was dressed in his uniform of white linen and denim. His hair was still pulled back in that lovely blond ponytail, the little diamond glinting from one ear. His face was unshaven, several days' stubble on his cheeks and chin, and he looked tired, the skin beneath his eyes smudged.

She wanted to smile graciously and act as if it was just an old friend dropping by, but her voice had deserted her and her cool had long since fled. His eyes, the green glinting in the hazel, seemed to bore into her and silently she stepped back, letting him enter.

He seemed about to speak but when his lips parted, no sound issued. Instead he opened his arms and she stepped into his embrace, feeling his warm cheek against her head, which was now covered in about an inch of hair that looked like a copper halo. They stood thus for a minute—or an hour—she wasn't certain. Aaron was there, in her apartment, in her arms! She could stand there forever—it was enough. She felt something warm and wet on her forehead and realized it was a tear!

"Aaron, what is it?"

"Oh, Marissa! I'm so sorry." His arms tightened around her and she stayed perfectly still, feeling he might disappear if she moved. "I was afraid, Marissa. I didn't know my own heart. But I found you! I'm so glad. I'm, God, I don't know what I am." Pulling back, he laughed, though the tears were still in his eyes and he blushed, shattering her image of him as master of all he surveyed, making him suddenly human and thus even more endearing.

Leading him to her couch, she pulled him down next to her. She wanted to demand why he was here, why he had deserted her, why he had failed to be her prince charming, but these past weeks, the training then the loss, the new start, had changed Marissa. She was able to do something she wouldn't have been able to do just a short while ago. She was able to wait. To be patient and give him a chance to speak. He was here—it was enough.

His large hand smoothed her cheek, a finger tracing the cheekbone, the bridge of her nose. He smiled, though his eyes were still sad as he stroked the soft thatch of hair on her head. "I'm sorry, Marissa. I wanted to tame you. To humble you, to make you change. I didn't understand then that you were perfect. Just as you were—as you are. I'm sorry."

Her hands flew to her head. Then she laughed. "For this? Don't be. It might be the best thing that ever happened to me. I was vain, Aaron. God, you must have seen that, that's why you did it! I lived on my looks and my hair was my signature, I guess you'd say. I feel so free now, Aaron! I was so wrapped up in all that, I came to believe it was all I was. I lost me, Aaron. I lost me."

"And now you're found?" he asked gently, looking around her small apartment.

"Well, yes! I guess so. I'm enrolled at NYU and I'm majoring in art history. Me! In college, can you believe it! I'm going to support myself and learn about things I love."

"And Tom?" Aaron's voice was casual but his hands were clenched in his lap.

"We met once. I tried to give the money back but I didn't really try, if I'm honest. He said to please keep it because he wanted me to have it! He's even richer than I thought! When I protested the amount, he told me it was less than one percent of his net worth! Can you imagine! He said what we had was worth that to him, at the least. I think he felt guilty about it, you know. About dumping me and not even having the guts to tell me face-to-face. So who am I to stand in the way of someone's penance?" She grinned, her eyes glinting mischievously and Aaron smiled back, his eyes lighting up for the first time.

"So, Aaron. What about you? How did you get away from your busy training schedule? Shouldn't you be whipping some submissive girl about now or watching her suck off one of your house slaves?" Marissa tried to keep her voice light but the bitterness seeped through and she turned away.

"I quit."

"What?"

"I quit. Retired. I'm not a trainer anymore. I'm done."

"Why?" she whispered. Her heart was singing, soaring, doing loop-de-loops inside of her.

"I don't know. I'd had enough, I guess. I'm ready for something new." He paused, as if he had been about to say something, but stopped himself. Their eyes met and though nothing was said, suddenly everything was understood.

"Marissa, I don't want to take you by force. I don't want to be your trainer. I don't want to trick you into wanting me because you want the control I offer. I want you on your own terms. I want you for who you are, not for how gracefully you submit to a whipping, or how sexually adept you are or even how beautiful you are.

"I want you because you are Marissa. Because, I fell in love with your wild spirit, with your essence, with you. I didn't mean to, and God knows I tried not to, and it took me all this time to finally bloody admit it and accept my own feelings. I'm a bloody idiot, and I would completely understand if you want nothing more to do with me. I'm just some jerk who used his position of power over you to steal a kiss and to manipulate your feelings. I love you, but I expect nothing in return. Truly I don't. I just wanted you to know."

"Aaron!" She had to deny it, to explain how wrong he was, but his words were echoing and dancing in her head, preventing her for a moment from speaking. *I want you because you are Marissa. I love you.* Dreams she'd thought she'd put to rest leaped back full-blown in a blaze of delirious glory. Finally she found her tongue. "Aaron, you stupid man! How could you not know how much I love you! How could you not have known it then? You broke my heart, but now you've mended it!"

Aaron stood up slowly, looking down at Marissa who was smiling beatifically though her dark eyes pooled with tears. He didn't respond but his eyes were smoldering, a fire lit from within. Slowly, his eyes locked on her, he unbuttoned his shirt and let it drop. His shoulders were broad and his chest was hard and lean, dark blond curls in a V on firm flesh. His pants rode low on his hips and his stomach was flat, a little line of dark blond hair disappearing down from his navel into his pants.

Holding out his hand to Marissa, he silently commanded her to stand in front of him, which she did. Marissa was dressed simply for an evening at home of solitary study. She was wearing an oversized T-shirt and cutoff jeans shorts as it was still warm in mid-September in the city, and she had no air-conditioning.

"Lift your arms," he said quietly, and she did.

Slowly he lifted the T-shirt, taking it off, leaving her only in the little shorts, her braless, high, round breasts exposed. "Attention," he whispered, and Marissa's face softened, as if she was entering some kind of trance. Her lips parted and she stared in the distance, her chin lifted. She lifted her shoulders, causing her breasts to jut out prettily. Her nipples hardened under his gaze.

"Kneel up." Gracefully she lowered herself to the hardwood floor. "Hands behind your head." As she obeyed, Aaron stepped out of his jeans and slid his underwear down and off. His cock was fully erect, the tip glistening.

Their gazes locked as Aaron moved forward, bringing the head of his cock to her mouth. No demure slave girl with eyes on the floor. Instead Marissa grinned and opened wide, savoring the lovely silken texture of his steel-hard manhood as it slid into her mouth. She drew back slightly, teasing the tip, making him moan, pulling back as he thrust forward.

"Marissa," he moaned, his voice aching with need. Her name on his tongue was like water to her parched heart. This wasn't the trainer "teaching" her. She was the mistress here, no mistaking it, and lovingly she exercised her control until he cried her name again, grabbing her head and spurting his life seed into her willing mouth.

Now he knelt next to her, taking her in his arms. Their mouths met, lips desperately seeking each other, tongues entwining, sweet whispers escaping between kisses. She wanted to tell him how she had longed for him. How she had waited for him, feeling the need for him as palpable as the need for water. How she had died inside, giving up, despairing of him. And then, somehow, come alive again. How she had truly let go and somehow freed herself from that desperate need. How she only *wanted* him now—didn't *need* him—and how freeing that was. But she said nothing, it was all conveyed in her kiss, and in his response.

She felt his spirit, his longing for her, and it was powerful but she wasn't afraid. It was like a thunderstorm or the splendor of a rising wind far out at sea—dangerous and overwhelmingly beautiful. When he slipped down, unzipping her little shorts, pushing down her now soaked panties, she stopped thinking altogether, her mind a blissful blank of raw sensation. When his tongue found her center she mewled like a tiny kitten, feeling a rush of pleasure so keen she actually lost consciousness for a few brief moments.

Then his mouth was on hers again, reviving her with his kisses, the taste of her own sex on his lips, mingling with the hint of his seed still in her mouth. Lifting her in his arms, Aaron carried Marissa to her bed, dropping her onto the soft down quilt, falling on top of her, his renewed need making him impatient.

Lifting her hands high over her head, Aaron held Marissa's wrists down as if she might struggle against him. She thrilled to his strong hands holding her down. Lifting her pelvis, spreading her legs in clear invitation, she delighted in his hard cock pressing against her opening.

"Fuck me, fuck me," she begged, and this time he did, pressing himself into her soft, yielding body, gripping her wrists hard, forcing her legs further apart with his own strong thighs.

"I want you," he said, his voice low and urgent. "I want you."

"Yes," she breathed, arching into him, her body hot against his, melting into him. He fucked her hard and fast, the days and weeks of pent-up need spending themselves against her. He would have taken her now whether or not she wanted it—he would have raped her if he had to. Oh, but he didn't. She wanted this onslaught, this delicious invasion, with every fiber of her being.

His cock felt so perfect, completely filling her. She didn't want to close her eyes, she wanted to keep them on his beautiful face as he loomed over her, thrusting hard into her, whispering her name like a prayer. Against her will, her eyes fluttered shut. She was almost over the edge when he pulled up and sat back on his knees, his cock perpendicular to his belly and glistening with her juices.

"Turn over. Get up, on your knees," he commanded, his voice hoarse. She scrambled to obey and he knelt behind her, guiding himself into her, gently at first. Holding her hips, he began to thrust in and out of her pussy, pulling almost all the way out before slamming hard against her, making her grunt with the impact.

"You," he said, thrusting, "belong—" again a thrust, hard, to punctuate each word "—to—" she groaned with pleasure "—me." Then his tempo increased as he moved hard and fast inside her.

"Oh, my God, Jesus God, help me, oh, my God," she cried, her words rising in pitch as he carried her along with him over the precipice of an orgasm so blindingly intense she collapsed beneath him, unable to move for several moments.

Aaron fell with her and slowly rolled away from her, their sticky bodies parting, the air cool against their heat. Marissa became aware of her own breathing, still jagged, as her heart continued to pound against her ribs. Aaron lay next to her, his hand flung across her back, his other hand under his head. Slowly she turned toward him and lifted herself onto one elbow.

God, he was so beautiful, lying there in his naked perfection, all long, lean muscles and that gorgeous cock now at half-mast, looking innocent and in need of kisses. She snuggled against him, whispering shyly, "Hi."

He smiled, turning to face her, kissing her mouth lightly and said in return, "Hi there." They laughed and he drew the sheets up over them as the drying sweat on their bodies had chilled them. When Marissa awoke, he was still there—it hadn't been a dream.

She didn't notice it at first. The little trunk was hidden behind boxes of old bills and piles of mildewed clothing that looked as though they hadn't been disturbed since World War II. Nicole was exhausted—she'd been going through her grandmother's old things all morning, and so far it had been tedious and sad. Did a person's whole life really come down to a few dusty boxes in the attic?

She felt tears well again as she thought of her grandmother, who she would never see again. Nana, as she had called her, had died the month before. She had only been seventy-two, and her daughter, Nicole's mother, had found her accidentally when she dropped by to bring a casserole. Nana had passed away sitting on her sofa, a romance novel still in her hand. She looked entirely peaceful, as if she'd merely fallen asleep. Pop had passed away only the prior year from a massive heart attack at the age of seventy-nine.

"Would you go through her things?" Nicole's mother had begged her. "I just can't face it." The twenty-five-year-old was an obedient girl, even though she was all grown up and lived on her own in an apartment in town.

Nicole agreed to do as her mother had asked, spending the day packing boxes for charity and boxes to review later with her sisters, full of old photo albums and various memorabilia. Nicole and Nana had been especially close, and Nicole thought she knew everything there was to know about her grandmother.

Nicole might not have noticed the small trunk, more of a strongbox really, but something about it caught her eye. Underneath the dust, it was silver. Aluminum, in fact, and sturdily built. And it was locked. Pushing aside the piles of junk, she scooted over to the trunk. She pulled at the little lock but it didn't give.

The ringing phone downstairs drew her away.

"Winston residence," she said, slightly out of breath.

"Elizabeth." The voice was deep and resonant. Nicole was startled and confused for a moment. Who was calling who was so familiar as to use her grandmother's first name, but not familiar enough to know she had died?

"Excuse me, who's calling?"

"Forgive me, I thought you were Elizabeth. Is she available, please?"

"Oh, dear," Nicole's voice wavered, hating to impart the news to someone who obviously didn't know. "Who is this, please?"

The man seemed to hesitate, but, perhaps sensing something amiss, as Nicole's grandmother had lived alone since her husband's death, answered, "This is James Stevenson. An old friend. I'm afraid I've been out of the country for some months. Is she all right?"

"I'm sorry, Mr. Stevenson, to be the bearer of bad news, but my grandmother passed away last month. She died peacefully in her sleep." Tears sprang to her eyes, and she tried to keep her voice steady as she spoke to the stranger, who might now be dealing with his own grief.

"I'm sorry," he said, his voice suddenly cracking. "Thank you." Nicole heard the click of his receiver and she gently cradled her own. She sat thinking for a while, wondering who the stranger with the deep voice was, who had obviously known Nana well enough to call, and in such a familiar way, and yet, hadn't known of her death. James Stevenson. An old friend. The name seemed familiar, and yet Nicole couldn't quite place it.

Perhaps she should call him back, offer him some comfort. She could view his number on the call log of the phone, if she chose to. But no, she decided. She would leave the man to his privacy. Whatever his relationship had been with Nana, it was clear he was shocked and saddened by the news. Leave him time to process his grief.

Nicole's eyes filled with tears for the hundredth time that weekend, as her gaze fell on a photograph of Nana and Pop. It was from early in their marriage, sometime in the '50s. The picture was black and white, but by the shading and light, one could see that Nana, of course then only known as Elizabeth, had fair hair and fair skin. She was smiling, the big happy smile of someone young and in love. Her face was turned slightly toward her husband, who stared directly at the camera, his expression self-conscious and stiff as he posed for the lens.

Elizabeth, though, seemed unaware of the camera. Her hair was pulled back in a careless ponytail, tendrils of unruly hair blowing gently against her cheek. Her face looked fresh and open. A Kansas farm girl kind of freshness, with a little sprinkling of freckles across her broad snubbed nose.

Nicole held the little photo, one she'd looked at many times before, and mentally compared herself with the woman she saw there. Nana was younger even than she in that old picture. Where Elizabeth was blonde and freckled, Nicole was darker with dark brown hair and hazel eyes that changed from green to gray depending on her outfit or her mood. Nicole's was a more delicate face, with high fine cheekbones and eyes almost too large for her face. Her mouth was small, but the lips were generous and even sensual. She had always envied her Nana's open, natural good looks, unaware of her own passion which lurked, waiting, behind those gray-green eyes.

Next to the photo were several lovely seashells, their horny exteriors protecting the delicate, milky pink curves inside. Nicole lifted a nautilus shell, cradling it gently in her hands. It brought back sharp memories of summers spent collecting shells at dawn, while everyone else but she and Nana slept. The world had seemed to belong only to the two of them then. Nicole sighed loudly, wiping a tear from her cheek. Everything about this old house was steeped in memories of Nana and Pop. She needed to get the hell out of there and home to her little cat George.

Nicole found her mind drifting back to the little strongbox in the attic. She found it had seized her imagination. What was in there that it had to be kept locked? And where was the key?

Enjoy this excerpt from
Sacred Circle
© Copyright Claire Thompson, 2005

Robert Dalton — Elder, Coven of the Red Covenant. It was neatly inscribed on one side of the card. On the other, in a thin angular scrawl he had written, *124 Charles Street. Saturday, 9:00 p.m.* Beneath it was a telephone number.

Grace fingered the little card. It was printed on fine, heavy stock, the lettering engraved in embossed shiny red. She was lying in her daybed, staring out the window. Her room was hot, despite the best efforts of the ceiling fan overhead. The little window-unit air conditioner in the adjoining room was wheezing its best effort to cool the place, but the tropical summer balm of New Orleans won out.

Grace sat in her panties and bra, her elegant black dress and high-heeled sandals tossed aside. Lifting her heavy French braid, she piled it on top of her head a moment, letting the wet breeze from her open window blow gently against her neck. The thick, waxy leaves of the magnolia tree outside her window were dripping with the recent rain shower. She'd just missed getting wet as she hurried home from the party, her mind reeling, her heart racing.

Why was she acting this way? It certainly wasn't Robert Dalton. While reasonably attractive—he was not her type. She preferred a more restrained sort of person. Someone more modest and less ostentatious.

No, it wasn't the man.

It was what he had offered.

She knew it was ridiculous. Why was she now suddenly allowing adolescent fantasies to run amuck in her head this way? She'd held such a tight rein for so long on feelings she had almost come to believe were nothing more than the feverish imagination of a young girl.

What had he said? "To spill a little of life's essence." Yes! That's what she felt now. A desperate longing for some of that promised "essence". Her own essence was flattened, she felt—a dried and sputtering spirit, left starving and hollow from years of denial and neglect. His one whisper of the chance for blood had set her body trembling, aching for it.

Yet, surely it was all a game? How could it be more? What was wrong with her? Had she read so many tomes about the creatures of the night that now she actually believed she was one? Ridiculous! Even if they did still exist, surely she would have known such a thing about herself. It would have manifested itself before now. Where were her fangs? The elongated canines reported in legend and exploited in Hollywood movies?

Parting her lips, gingerly she touched the pointed little teeth that could pierce skin and sinew with ease, if she were a real vampire. Lifting a thin white wrist, she bit gently against it, wondering what it would be like to actually puncture another's flesh. To pierce the vein and watch the glorious red tide flow from it, waiting for her special kiss. Was it her imagination, or did her canine teeth suddenly seem longer, sharper?

A bottle of wine stood next to her bed. A half-full bottle of cabernet sauvignon she'd grabbed from the kitchen counter on her way to her bed. She pulled out the cork and poured a glass. Lifting the glass goblet, she tilted her head back to take a long, deep drink, savoring its sweet burn.

Grace sighed, the image of a pale throat offered sliding unbidden into her consciousness, even as her fingers slipped down to her panties. She finished the glass and poured another, drinking it quickly. She realized she wanted to be drunk. To give herself permission in this way to do what she knew she was about to do.

So tight had been her own censorship of her true feelings that she rarely allowed herself the fantasy that was now stealthily easing its way into her brain. That pale throat, bared for her. Dark black hair curled in tendrils around it. The throat was strong, sinewy with corded muscle. It was a man's throat. Whose it was did not matter. It was an image that had floated through her dreams many times before.

Only now did she allow it to come through her conscious thought. She focused on it, imagining the face that would go with such a sensual and exposed throat. A strong jaw, a cruel mouth, but softened when it smiled. Lips ruby red, parting, revealing the elongated canines of her lover...

Her lover! Grace's fingers found their mark now, pushing aside the silky fabric of her panties. Her pussy was wet, eager for her touch. She rubbed and swirled in little arcs against her sex, moving toward the center and then away, wishing it was someone else's touch.

The wine coursed through her veins, giving her permission to explore the secret fantasy more fully. Recalling a half-forgotten dream, Grace closed her eyes. The dream brightened — its colors and feelings vivid in her mind's eye. It became more real than her narrow daybed in her small apartment, or her simple, rather dull life. For just that moment she didn't feel weak or in pain.

She could almost smell her lover now — the scent of exotic lemony spices and heat she'd experienced at the Vampire Ball. The lover of her dreams — with his dark hair and cruel smile.

They were naked, lying together on a large featherbed in the middle of a dark warm forest. He was leaning up on one elbow, kissing her hair, her forehead, her cheekbones, her lips. Slowly she felt his soft mouth edge down toward her throat.

Her golden auburn hair was loose around her head. She moved it herself, giving him access, desperate for what he was going to do. *Yes*, she thought now, *yes, do it. Take me. Claim me. I want it.* Grace moaned aloud as she rubbed herself, slipping a finger into her cunt as the dream image of her lover bit her neck, making her gasp.

He suckled at her throat, pressing his long body against hers. She shifted, her mouth watering, as she smelled her own blood on his lips. Silently she told him it was her turn, and he lay back, baring his own throat for her. She leaned over, dropping her head down, covering his face with her hair as she licked his supple flesh. In her fantasy she bit down, while in real life she only moaned, writhing against her own fingers, the sweet rusty taste of blood almost real to her.

As her sharp little teeth pierced the flesh, the impossibly rich red blood gushed like two little fountains of life against her mouth. She pulled back, trying to catch the flow, not wanting to waste a drop of his essence. It tasted better than anything she'd ever experienced in real life. It was more than drink, more than food. It went beyond mere sustenance. It was, quite literally, her life's blood.

Oh! It felt so real, just for that moment.

With a cry she came, jerking in uncontrollable little spasms, as her fingers drew out the last bit of pleasure. She fell on her side and her hand flew out to steady herself, knocking the bottle of wine from its perch, and onto her white sheets. The wine spread in a dark red pool. Grace didn't see—she was asleep, lost in blood-drenched dreams.

About the author:

Claire Thompson has written numerous novels and short stories, all exploring aspects of Dominance & submission. Ms. Thompson's gentler novels seek not only to tell a story, but to come to grips with, and ultimately exalt in the true beauty and spirituality of a loving exchange of power. Her darker works press the envelope of what is erotic and what can be a sometimes dangerous slide into the world of sadomasochism. She writes about the timeless themes of sexuality and romance, with twists and curves to examine the 'darker' side of the human psyche. Ultimately Claire's work deals with the human condition, and our constant search for love and intensity of experience.

Claire Thompson welcomes mail from readers. You can write to her c/o Ellora's Cave Publishing at 1056 Home Avenue, Akron OH 44310-3502.

Why an electronic book?

We live in the Information Age—an exciting time in the history of human civilization in which technology rules supreme and continues to progress in leaps and bounds every minute of every hour of every day. For a multitude of reasons, more and more avid literary fans are opting to purchase e-books instead of paperbacks. The question to those not yet initiated to the world of electronic reading is simply: *why?*

1. *Price.* An electronic title at Ellora's Cave Publishing runs anywhere from 40-75% less than the cover price of the <u>exact same title</u> in paperback format. Why? Cold mathematics. It is less expensive to publish an e-book than it is to publish a paperback, so the savings are passed along to the consumer.

2. *Space.* Running out of room to house your paperback books? That is one worry you will never have with electronic novels. For a low one-time cost, you can purchase a handheld computer designed specifically for e-reading purposes. Many e-readers are larger than the average handheld, giving you plenty of screen room. Better yet, hundreds of titles can be stored within your new library—a single microchip. (Please note that Ellora's Cave does not endorse any specific brands. You can check our website at www.ellorascave.com for customer recommendations we make available to new consumers.)

3. *Mobility.* Because your new library now consists of only a microchip, your entire cache of books can be taken with you wherever you go.

4. *Personal preferences are accounted for.* Are the words you are currently reading too small? Too large? Too...ANNOYING? Paperback books cannot be modified according to personal preferences, but e-books can.

5. *Innovation.* The way you read a book is not the only advancement the Information Age has gifted the literary community with. There is also the factor of what you can read. Ellora's Cave Publishing will be introducing a new line of interactive titles that are available in e-book format only.

6. *Instant gratification.* Is it the middle of the night and all the bookstores are closed? Are you tired of waiting days—sometimes weeks—for online and offline bookstores to ship the novels you bought? Ellora's Cave Publishing sells instantaneous downloads 24 hours a day, 7 days a week, 365 days a year. Our e-book delivery system is 100% automated, meaning your order is filled as soon as you pay for it.

Those are a few of the top reasons why electronic novels are displacing paperbacks for many an avid reader. As always, Ellora's Cave Publishing welcomes your questions and comments. We invite you to email us at service@ellorascave.com or write to us directly at: 1056 Home Avenue, Akron OH 44310-3502.

NEED A MORE EXCITING
WAY TO PLAN YOUR DAY?

ELLORA'S
CAVEMEN

2006 CALENDAR

COMING THIS FALL

THE
ELLORA'S CAVE
LIBRARY

Stay up to date with Ellora's Cave Titles
in Print with our Quarterly Catalog.

TO RECIEVE A CATALOG,
SEND AN EMAIL WITH YOUR NAME
AND MAILING ADDRESS TO:

CATALOG@ELLORASCAVE.COM
OR SEND A LETTER OR POSTCARD
WITH YOUR MAILING ADDRESS TO:
CATALOG REQUEST
C/O ELLORA'S CAVE PUBLISHING, INC.
1337 COMMERCE DRIVE #13
STOW, OH 44224

Discover for yourself why readers can't get enough of the multiple award-winning publisher Ellora's Cave. Whether you prefer e-books or paperbacks, be sure to visit EC on the web at www.ellorascave.com for an erotic reading experience that will leave you breathless.

www.ellorascave.com

Printed in the United States
46535LVS00001B/163-192